W9-AHF-901

DogBreath
Victorious

DogBreath Victorious

Chad Henry

HOLIDAY HOUSE / NEW YORK

This book is dedicated to:
Bruce, first and always
My parents and family
A. M., of course, sine qua non
the Glickfield Irregulars
Linda in spite of everything
and to the memory of Ellie Wetzel—
mentor, friend, bright star

Library of Congress Cataloging-in-Publication Data
Henry, Chad.
DogBreath victorious / by Chad Henry.—1st ed.
p.   cm.
Summary: DogBreath, Tim's alternative Seattle grunge rock band,
enters a major battle of the bands contest, but is beaten by
The Angry Housewives.
ISBN 0-8234-1458-2
[1. Rock music—Fiction.   2. Mothers and sons—Fiction.
3. Seattle—Fiction.]   I. Title.
PZ7.H39357Do   1999   99-19708
[Fic]—dc21   CIP

Chapter One

I guess the trouble started—bang, kapow— the day I brought home the flyer advertising the Battle of the Bands contest at Lewd Fingers'. Me and my band, DogBreath, starring me, Tim Threlfall, on lead guitar and lead vocals, and Ziggy Jones on drums, well, we'd been working hard to get a break in show business, but when you're in high school, it's not so easy to get gigs. Especially not paying gigs. Especially not in Seattle. Even when you're very mature for your age.

And I needed the money. Really bad. Because, unfortunately, six months ago, my dad died. He was only an insurance salesman, but I have to say I really miss him. Still, he didn't leave me and Mom anything but a heavily mortgaged house, a Montego four-door with electric windows and mag wheels, and a lot of bills. An insurance salesman with no life insurance.

That's what my lit teacher, Mrs. Cederberg, would call irony. At first I thought she was saying "ironing," but Mrs. Cederberg explained that there is no ironing in literature, only irony, so a person should learn to recognize it. Just in case you don't have your dictionary nearby, here's Webster's definition, third one from the top:

Irony. Noun: a combination of circumstances or a result that is the opposite of what is, or might be, expected or considered appropriate.

My mom has no skills to speak of, so to prevent us from starving to death and being thrown out into the snow, I got a pizza delivery job at Mah-Jongg Pizza. Then, in an incident I won't go into in detail, the police suspended my driver's license for speeding. Like if you're going one mile over the speed limit you're like some mass murderer.

So, money, or its absence anyway, was a big issue around our house. Our lifestyle before Dad died was very what Ziggy calls "boozhy"—short for (I hope I can spell this right)—bourgeois, meaning: boring, pedestrian, unimaginative, middle-class, philistine, suburban, anti-art, pro-Fascist, TV-addicted couch potatoes. When Dad was around it was breakfast at 7:30, evenings in front of the TV, weekends washing the car, hosing the driveway, mowing the lawn, and visiting Grandma in the assisted care unit. With Dad gone, though the schedule has changed, we still have many of the finer things in life, Mom and me—only now we can't afford them anymore.

On top of death and poverty, I'd been heavily obsessing on Suzie Blethins, this girl at school who I loved who hated me. I couldn't sleep, couldn't eat, couldn't concentrate on anything because I loved her so heavily. I knew if our band was more famous, she might warm up to me a little bit.

But famous is not what we were. If there is a Black Hole of Fame, DogBreath was in it. Sure, the Dixy Lee Ray High School Entertainment Committee was real happy to have us play for free at Friday afternoon school dances. And then my aunt Shirley got us a job playing at Seattle Center for a senior citizens' dance. But we had to wear suits and disguise our hair and take the rings out of our noses and nipples and play stuff like "Strangers in the Night" and "Camptown Races," while all these geriatric cases were doing the merengue and the cha-cha-cha.

We earned a grand total of forty bucks for that gig. To add insult to anonymity, somebody ripped off my new fuzz pedal when we were taking out a load of gear to Ziggy's 1973 purple VW Beetle, Veronica. Todi and Flipper, our other two member guys, were so disgusted and demoralized, they quit on us. Ten bucks for a day of humiliation and frustration and a broken-up band. And I thought the music biz was supposed to be all glamour and groupies and James Dean Left-Bank stuff. I was wrong.

Anyway, the day this whole psycho catastrophe started was a Friday. School had been relentless all day. In first period biology, Mrs. Paden peered at us over her bifocals, smiled, and sang out in her piercing soprano, "Pop quiz on the nuke-you-lus, everyone!"

Guess who forgot to study. All quarter.

Then, in the hall at lunch, Suzie Blethins, she who I was dyingly in love with, she who made my heart sing, well, she made barfing motions in my general direction. *Barfing* motions!

In third period, Mrs. Lewis, the music teacher (and one of my mother's best friends) gave me a D minus on my song "Toe Jamming."

"This song is repetitious, Timmy," she said.

"It's supposed to be. That's the whole point," I said. "Life is repetitious. School is repetitious. Art should mirror life."

"Right on!" croaked Ziggy.

"Write a better song," Mrs. Lewis said.

I and Ziggy ran down the hallway at the end of third period, hoping to get to the Nihilists' Table at lunch. Mr. Thompson, the Boys' Club counselor (whether you want to be or not, you're automatically a member of the Boys' Club if you're even *suspected* of being male) yanked me into his office.

There I sat, squirming on the plastic couch, practically boiling with sweat. The smell of chalk dust and Pine-Sol hung in the air.

Mr. Thompson took a chair, looked at me like he was an undertaker and I was a corpse, and said, "Tim, I understand how hard it is on a young man when he loses his father suddenly. It must have been a terrible shock for you when he passed away with no warning."

"Yeah," I said. "My mom said she should never have showed him the bills before dinner."

"My father died when I was a young man, too," said Mr. Thompson. "I empathize, I do. But acting out this way—your hostility, bad grades, poor attitude, bizarre grooming—that's not going to bring your father back. You'd want him to be proud of you, wouldn't you?"

"Dad was an insurance salesman," I said. "I'm an artist. My dad wasn't proud of me before he died, I don't know why he would be proud of me now. He didn't understand me."

"I'm sure your father loved you, even if he didn't show it. Although he, like me, probably would have preferred that you didn't go around wearing motorcycle leathers and shaving the sides of your head and dyeing your hair black and pink and letting it hang in your eyes and stick out all over your head like a haystack."

Of course, Mr. Thompson barely has any hair himself. What he does have, he parts down by the top of his ear, then combs over his bald spot on top, like he thinks nobody can tell.

"My appearance is a professional choice, Mr. Thompson. I am the leader of an alternative rock band. Our name is DogBreath. Our public expects us to look this way," I said. (This was a deliberate exaggeration. We didn't have a public yet, but there was no reason to tell Thompson that.)

"Your mother is still unemployed, isn't she, Tim?" Thompson asked. "Does she know about your problems here?"

"No, my problems are my business. I am staying in school for my mother's sake. But I plan to be a multimillionaire rock star before I am twenty-five years old. School is meaningless to me, okay?"

"Well, Timmy," Mr. Thompson said in his most smarmiest tones, "I'm afraid I'm going to have to recommend to your mother that you stop all your band activities until your grades, your attitude, and your appearance improve drastically. I'll also recommend that you spend a minimum of eight hours in counseling with our wonderful school psychologist, Marjorie Mamet. And, of course, you'll be barred from playing music on the school premises, too."

"You're going to banish my band? *And* tell my mother?" I asked, not believing my ears.

"I have no other choice," he said. "And if I hear that you are disregarding me, I will be compelled to recommend you be suspended from school and given an incomplete grade. Of course that probably won't bother you, seeing that you're going to be a millionaire rock star, et cetera."

"What a bunch of Nazis," I yelled.

I stomped out of the Boys' Club office. I was crying a little. I'm not ashamed. Men should show their emotions. And after all, this was probably the second worst day of my life so far.

So you can appreciate why I was in a suicidal mood as I got on the bus after school. I was muttering to myself, "School is hell. Life is hell. School is a metaphor for life."

"No swearing on the bus, Threlfall."

Jean, our sado/maso/psycho-killer forty-five-year-old bus driver slitted her eyes at me. She was a vision in ancient acne scars, a modified Whoopi Goldberg hairdo, and a red nylon windbreaker that said "The Bowling

Banshees" across the back. She wore Evel Knievel driving gloves and kept a set of brass knuckles dangling from the rearview mirror.

"You hear me, Threlfall?" she repeated.

"It won't happen again, Jean," I lied.

I slumped into an empty seat, inhaling diesel fumes, trapped in this completely dark mental morass, thinking about how grody school is, when I was totally struck by inspiration. *School is hell.* Hell School, I thought. What a great song title. I will sing of my angst to the uncaring world.

I grabbed my notebook and started writing lyrics like crazy:

They make you take these classes
That no one ever passes,
And all the teachers come from the Twilight Zone.
Nah, nah, nah, nah nah!

Phoebe Fortiere, this very geeky blond girl with blue plastic cat glasses, came clumping down the aisle of the bus. She flopped down next to me and looked over at my notebook. She smelled of rose oil or something like that.

"What is that supposed to be," she whined through her adenoids. "A poem?"

"I am writing lyrics, if you knew anything," I quipped.

"Oh, my God, you're a lyricist?" Phoebe gasped out.

Just then, Jean, the lady bus driver, turned on the ignition and released the air brakes. Suddenly, the air was ripped by an Indigenous Abo-American-like war cry. My best friend and drummer, Ziggy, came screeching onto the bus, barely making it inside alive as the hydraulic doors almost crushed his tall, bony frame. He came loping down the aisle toward me, waving a yellow flyer.

"Timmy! Timmy, my man! Check it out! DogBreath is made! Look at this thing! We are thousand-aires!"

Chapter Two

Ziggy's always late getting on the bus after school because he has to change out of his dress back into his regular clothes. Maybe I should explain—back when this all happened, in Seattle it was considered very freeing amongst some of the really outer-limits rock culture music guys to wear dresses or skirts, usually with combat boots and thermal underwear. It's what Kurt did. But parental hysteria being what it is, Ziggy's dad wouldn't let him wear dresses to school, so Ziggy hid dresses in his girlfriend Natasha's locker, then changed into them when he got there. You can imagine it drove Mr. Thompson completely non compos mentis.

So, here came Ziggy going x-million miles per hour down the bus aisle. He hurled himself into the seat next to me, exhaling mass quantities of cigarette smoke, whoosh, and knocking Phoebe, who he forgot to notice, to the floor, but Ziggy never looks where he's going. He shoved this crumpled, dirty, greasy sheet of paper in my face.

"Read this, Timmer! It's us! It's karma!" he crowed. The flyer read:

Rad Band Contest @ Lewd Fingers' Dirt Club!! Next Saturday night!! Come one, come all!! Punk, Post Punk, Pop, Retro Rock, Techno-Rap, Art Rock, Garage Band, Hip Hop, Be Bop, House, Alternative Metal, Grunge, you name it!! Talent, experience not a requirement. Entry fee— 50 per band. Let's get ugly and bang our heads and achieve god-realization through Modern Music!! Sponsored by Chainsaw Music and Radio Station KRAP. First Prize Two Thousand Dollars U.S. PLUS audition for big Chainsaw Records recording contract!!!

"Two thousand dollars?" I asked.

"It's *us*, man, it's DogBreath," Ziggy gurgled. "Our name is written all over this. You and me, we're goin' to your house, we're callin' Todi and Flipper to come over to DogBreath band practice!"

"Band practice?" I began. "Wait. Zig, there's something I must tell you. . . ."

He leaned over and asked Phoebe, "Hey, man, what are you doing on the floor?" Then, turning back to me, he explained, "Tim, my man, at long last, the break we've been waiting for—a chance for DogBreath to triumph!"

"Well," I said. "I've got some bad news and some bad news. What do you want first?"

"Geez," Ziggy said. "I guess the bad news."

"The bad news is, Mr. Thompson of the Boys' Club Thompsons just told me that I have to stop playing in the band until my grades get better."

"Never happen. What's the *bad* news?" Ziggy asked.

"The bad news is, he said if he finds out we're still playing, he'll get me suspended from school and I'll get all incompletes and drop out of school and wind up on public assistance."

"Timmy, it's a chance we've got to take. Are you gonna let that dink ruin your life? Lewd Fingers' Dirt Club is a major venue. Once we can play for some real actual human beings, there will be no stopping us! We'll go through the roof. We'll become legends in our own time!" He bounced up and down on the seat, his matted blond dreadlocks swinging all over the place.

I am a little more cautious by nature than Ziggy.

"Supposing I *do* decide to risk my entire future and continue this enterprise. Where are we going to get fifty dollars to join this contest?" I inquired politely.

"You're the leader of the band. You get it."

"Where am I supposed to get fifty bucks? *You* get it," I suggested.

"Get it from your mom, man," Ziggy said.

"We're so poor," I reminded him, "the mice are stoop-shouldered. My mom even kept the fifty dollars my grandma sent me for Christmas."

"That is child abuse, dude. You have a legal right to that money. Besides, if we win this contest, you can pay her back immédiatemente. I fail to see the problem. If you want to be our leader, you got to assume the responsibilities along with the privileges as my dad is so fond of telling me everytime I want to like do anything."

"Okay," I said. "I'll get the money. Somehow."

"Deal," said Ziggy.

"And I got a totally inspired idea for a new song. 'Hell School,' it's called. Help me finish writing the lyrics and by the time we get over to my house for band practice, we can learn it!" I started to sing:

"They make you take these classes
That no one ever passes,
And all the teachers come from the Twilight Zone.
Nah, nah, nah, nah nah!"

Then Ziggy added, in his hiccupy voice:

"They make you take hot showers
And read and write for hours. . . ."

Then Ziggy got stuck. ". . . *'and read and write for hours. And read and write for hours'*—dammit. I wish I didn't have such a headache. I can't think of this thought I'm tryin' to think of."

Phoebe stood in the aisle, hanging on to the pole and looking over our shoulders. She pushed Ziggy's dreadlocks out of the way so she could see the page. She looked at the paper.

"How about: 'First they rip your flesh, and then they eat your bones!'?" she suggested.

I and Ziggy looked at her with wonder. This weird, geeky-looking girl appeared to have a certain naive genius. I started to recite from the top of the lyric.

"They make you take these classes
That no one ever passes,
And all the teachers come from the Twilight Zone.
Nah, nah, nah, nah nah!
They make you take hot showers
And read and write for hours.
First they rip your flesh, and then they
Eat your bones!"

"Awesome! Superb!" hollered Ziggy. All three of us began to sing, in more or less the same melody:

"Hell School,
Lord, get me outta here.
Hell School,
No wearin' leather here.
Hell School—
It ain't pretty!"

Ziggy started jumping up and down on the seat. "It's beyond brilliant, dudes! A work of genius. Of true, startling, pure heartbreaking genius!"

He flopped back down and pulled out a cigarette from a crumpled pack of Camel straights and lit it.

"I got the drum pattern in my head already. It's perfect!"

The bus driver snatched up the hand microphone she uses for harassing her hapless prisoners/riders.

"Siegmund Jones, please extinguish all smoking materials while riding this bus or I'll rip your face off!"

"Hell School," Ziggy began to sing. "Hell School."

At that exact moment the bus came to a screeching halt at my stop.

"I said no swearing on this bus, dammit!" hollered Jean.

I and Ziggy bounded out of our seat with the thrill of inspiration. Phoebe started to sit down, but Ziggy grabbed her arm and yanked her down the aisle of the bus with us.

"What are you doing?" she wailed.

"You are coming with us to our band practice," Ziggy explained gently. "You are a genius and a weirdo and a beautiful singer and you are going to join DogBreath and make us wonderful."

"I am?" Phoebe replied, clumping up the aisle toward the door.

Jean snarled at us as we exited.

"Down, Jean," Ziggy commanded.

"You guys, I'm supposed to go to play practice," Phoebe said as Ziggy pulled her along behind.

Hopping down the treacherous steps of the bus, I turned to look at Ziggy.

"Hey, don't I have any say in this? I *am* the leader of this group. I should be in on the decision," I said.

"This is bigger than both of us," Ziggy whispered. "This is a decision already made for us out there somewhere in the cosmos. It's fate. Kismet. Karma. It's destiny. Don't fight it, dude."

"Okay," I said reluctantly. "But remember what Yoko Ono did to the Beatles."

I looked at Phoebe Fortiere, who was looking just as stunned as I felt. Standing there with her limp blond hair, and her blue plastic glasses and Junior Miss Nordstrom basement clothes, she looked to me like a hopeless boozh.

Chapter Three

On this particular fateful Friday I'm trying to tell you about, me and Ziggy and Phoebe bombed quietly through our front door, passed through the living room, where I threw down my books and the flyer for the contest. Ziggy headed down the basement stairs, clomp, clomp, three steps at a time really loud in his Frankenstein boots. Before Phoebe and I could get to the basement door, my mom came into the living room.

"My life is getting better and better. My life is getting better and better. Oh, hi, kids." Mom was chanting her affirmations. She'd been so depressed after Dad died, she couldn't even get out of bed for a long time. Then somebody sent her this book on positive thinking, and ever since, she's been the Affirmation Queen. She has them taped to the refrigerator and the bathroom mirror, and she listens to subliminal motivation tapes on her Walkman. It's fairly spooky.

I make fun of her affirmations. But underneath I'm

glad she discovered them. Because for a while there, I was *really, really concerned* about her mental health. She's not a very strong person.

She was all dressed up for once and had on some makeup dealie that covered up the dark circles under her eyes and a nice hairdo. She was putting some bridge mix into a bowl. Suddenly I looked at Mom hard. Something was different.

"Mom, your hair! How come you're all blond?"

"Oh, this? It's a wig! I decided it's time for me to *lighten up*! I've just been so depressed since your father passed. And I read in *Ladies Home Journal* that if you want a change, start with your hair. So—no more bummed-out brunette. Busy blondes have more fun! Do you like it?"

"Mom, you look gorge. Oh—Mom, Phoebe, Phoebe, Mom."

Phoebe stuck out her hand and said, "How do you do, Mrs. . . ."

I grabbed Phoebe's arm and yanked her toward the basement steps. "We gotta go downstairs now, Mom," I hollered over my shoulder.

"Stop *now,* Timmy. Thank you. Are you and your little friends going to watch television?" Mom asked.

"No, we're having band practice," I said.

"No, you're not, Tim. Mr. Thompson called me today. He told me everything."

"Mom, you're not going to make me stop the band?"

"Honey, you boys broke up anyway, didn't you?"

"Yeah, but now we're starting again."

"We'll have to discuss this later. I've invited a group of women over. I'd prefer that you didn't play music. You'll just have to watch television or play Perquackey or talk among yourselves."

"What are you doing with this group of women?" I asked.

"I am hostessing a Mary Kay party, dear."

"Mary Kay party? God, that is so lame!" I hollered. "If Ziggy or Todi or Flipper or anybody finds out, my credibility is shot! Why do you want to sell Mary Kay?"

"Because we need the money badly, Timmy. If we want to stay here in this house, and keep our car and so on, I have to get a job. Besides, Mary Kay has a wonderful philosophy of life. So I am going to try to sell Mary Kay cosmetics."

"Philosophy?" I said. "We're facing abrupt psychic death and suddenly you're talkin' philosophy?"

"My shamanism teacher says if you have a problem, don't dwell on it. Instead, form a mental image of what you really *want* to happen to you and surround it with a warm pink light. Mary Kay is very spiritually oriented. All her products are pink."

"That's wonderful," said Phoebe.

"Great idea, Mom," I said. "Gotta go."

"Okay, dear. Just remember, no band."

"Sure, Mom." I grabbed Phoebe and ran her down to the basement.

Behind us, I heard my mom chanting, "My life is getting better and better. My life is getting better and better."

I found myself starting to mutter the same thing, like a commercial jingle that you can't get out of your head.

My basement bedroom/rehearsal studio is really cool— there's rock band posters all over the place, and signs that we borrowed from around the neighborhood, like "ROAD WASHED OUT—DETOUR." And "EXTREMEST DANGER— HIGH VOLTAGE."

A year ago, I and Ziggy put up acoustical tile and more carpeting and stuff so DogBreath could practice without bothering anybody. At least I put it up while Zig made suggestions and took naps. It doesn't work too good, though. Mom's always sticking her head down the basement door and hollering, "Tim, turn it down! I can't hear myself *think!*" You'd think after a while she could come up with something original.

Phoebe followed me cautiously down the basement steps, and looked around very nervous like she was in the Chamber of Horrors at Madame Tussaud's Wax Museum (which Dad and Mom took me to when I was eight and it warped me for life).

"This place is really grim," she said. "How can you do art in an environment like this?"

"Art, schmart," I flung back at her.

Ziggy said, "Fear not, my shimmering goddess, my musette, Art practically lives here."

"Not today, it doesn't," I said. "Mom knows every-thing."

"So?" he said.

"She said we couldn't practice!" I said.

"It's imperative that we practice. This contest is too important, amigo. Are we not anarchists? If we are forced to employ deceit and subterfuge, so be it."

Ziggy grabbed the telephone. He wedged the receiver between his shoulder and ear while he rapped out drum patterns on his snare.

"Flipper, get over here immédiatemente. We have a date with destiny. Yeah, I'm talking about DogBreath. Look, you only think you quit. You're mistaken. Get over here. How does a million dollars sound to you? That's what I thought. Beat cheeks, man."

"A million bucks?" I inquired.

"We gotta have possibility thinking, Ythomit, my friend."

"Ythobit?" said Phoebe through her adenoids.

"Timothy spelled backward. Because that's what he is," explained Zig.

"It's not me, it's Mom. Zig, we can't practice while she's here, okay? We'll just talk."

"I don't think Todi and Flipper know how," said Zig, dialing the phone.

Phoebe started drifting around the room looking at posters and glancing through magazines.

I plugged in my Stratocaster, put on my headphones, turned up the volume, and hit a few power chords. I could still tell what Ziggy was saying, in spite of the headphones. He has distinctive lips—they're very easy to read.

"Todi, my main dude, we need you at DogBreath Central, pronto, on the double, et cetera. DogBreath lies quivering at the Brink of the Heroic Age of ÜberRock. Hop your board and thrash on over here."

Within about two minutes, Todi and Flipper, who both live in the neighborhood, came crashing ka-thunk, ka-thunk, down the basement steps.

"Tune in, turn on, drop out, fellow fellows," said Flipper.

"Don't worry, be happy," said Phoebe.

"Who's the babe?" Todi inquired, running a large hand across his carroty buzz cut.

"Fellow men, meet Phoebe," said Ziggy. "The next goddess of the known universe, soon to be revealed. Phoebe Fortiere, meet Todi and Flipper."

"Hi," Phoebe replied through her nose. She pulled a sketch pad and pencil from her book bag and got very busy drawing.

"Where'd you find her, selling Campfire mints?" Flipper said.

"Yeah, what's she supposed to be?" Todi insisted.

"Anything and everything," said Ziggy. "Camp follower, vocalist, poet, muse, inspiration, decoration—the hair of the dog of DogBreath."

"Do we have to split the money with her?" asked Flipper. Flipper's real name is Gordon Ishizuka. He's about six two, Asioid, weighs about two fifty, and has shoulder length green hair. He takes money at the Green Village II parking lot across the street from Uwajimaya. It's ruined him. Money's all he thinks about.

"Don't worry about money, worry about music, and the money will take care of itself," said Zig. "Now open your third eyes, gentlemen—Mister Tim has a new song, which we will now put together for the Lewd Fingers' extravaganza next Saturday night."

"Except I'm not allowed to practice, so we have to play really quiet, you guys."

"What's the point, man? Why are we even practicing if we can't play?" Flipper said.

Ziggy firmly closed the padded, carpeted door that led upstairs.

"We can practice the changes without cranking it. Plug in, pals," Ziggy said.

Todi and Flipper picked up bass guitar and keyboard, respectively. Ziggy twirled his drumsticks, as I worked out a chord pattern on my guitar.

"The name of the song is called 'Hell School.' Take it away, Tim!"

"Remember—quiet, you guys," I said.

"We'll be *so* quiet," Ziggy assured. He raised his drumsticks to count us in. "*Three, two, one, zero!*"

We worked on the song for the next half hour or so, very quietly. For the first ten or fifteen minutes, nobody could do anything right. Then Ziggy changed to another drum pattern, and Todi found some different chords in the bridge of the song, and everything seemed to drop into place as if by magic.

"Hell School, Lord get me outta here," I sang. And Phoebe chimed in with this strange harmony—well, you couldn't even call it harmony, really, she had this kind of fire engine wail that wasn't even in the same key we were singing in, but it was so bizarre that it was great. It gave the whole song this very eerie, hellacious quality. In the middle of the song, Todi and Flipper looked at Phoebe with something approaching respect.

We started to play faster, louder, more passionately. Ziggy was practically breaking his drumheads.

"I don't wanna go
Mama, don't make me go
Mama, please,
Mama, please,
Mama, nooooooo!!
Hell School"

I was singing like I'd never sung in my life, becoming one with my guitar, my microphone, swept away on a crashing wave of Art.

"Timmy! *Timmy!*"

Submerged in my peak experience, I vaguely became aware of another sound floating down the stairs.

"Timmy! Timmy! Are you practicing? I thought we agreed that you weren't going to—"

"We're playing CDs, Mom," I hollered.

"Then turn it down! Turn it down! Timmy! TURN IT DOWN!"

"Aw, crap," Ziggy sighed.

My mother came down through the basement door.

"Timmy, I'm trying to have a class up here," she said.

"Oh, that's all right, Mrs. Threlfall, you're not bothering us," said Ziggy, pounding on his drums. I hit him.

"Timmy, turn it down," she said. "I can't—"

"—hear myself think," I said at the same time as my mother.

"Don't get smart with me, young man," my mother requested in her most cornball manner. "Now please keep it quiet. I am trying to earn us a living up here." She turned around and headed up the steps. I followed her upstairs.

"Mom, can't we keep playing, I mean listening, for a while? We're having this like breakthrough."

"You'll have other breakthroughs. We have an agreement, Tim. Why don't you watch television or something for a while with your little friends?" she said.

"Get real, Mom. There's nothing on."

"Well, why don't you fix everybody a Pizzadog and some milk until our class is over."

I followed Mom into the living room. "Mom, we don't *want* a Pizzadog, we want to pract—"

I came through the living room door and stopped in my tracks. There were three of my mom's best friends sitting around the living room, towels turbaned onto their heads, and green gook drying all over their faces. Each of them had a TV tray in front of her with a bunch of makeup and cream and stuff set out.

"Oh, Bev, Timmy's getting so big!" said one of them through her green-gook mask. From the breathy clueless voice, I could tell it was Jetta Prince. She and her mom and her attorney husband and baby live over on Mercer Island and are even far more boozhier than Mom and me. "Tim, I bet you'd be really cute if you got a haircut!"

"Yeah, all the girls are crazy about him," said Mrs. Lewis, my music teacher. "What was that song you were playing, Timmy?" asked Mrs. Lewis.

"Hell School," I said.

"Hell School?" she wrinkled up her green nose.

"You inspired it, Mrs. Lewis," said Ziggy, who had just come through the basement door. He lumbered over.

"Hi, Ziggy," said one of the green faces. "It's me, Wendy."

"Hey, Wen. Timmy," he whispered to me, "get the fifty bucks before it's too late. Ask in front of other grown-ups. They hate being embarrassed in front of their friends," he advised, and clumped into the bathroom.

"Mom," I said. "I need fifty bucks."

"Not now, Tim," she said. "We're having a class. Ziggy, remember to put the seat back down when you're done!"

"But, Mom, this is important. It's for a band contest at Lewd Fingers' Dirt Club," I said.

Wendy, Mom's friend who works in the control tower in the university drawbridge—serious—said, "Hi, Tim! Haven't seen you and Ziggy at the bridge for a while. What's the Dirt Club?"

Mom said, "Oh, it's an underage disco or something."

"Mom, it's not a disco, it's a rock club. Look, could I have the fifty dollars now? I've gotta get back to prac—to entertain my friends."

"Tim, we just can't afford it right now. I can't even sell any of this Mary Kay stuff!"

"What about the fifty dollars Grandma sent me for my birthday?" I asked, getting desperate.

"Honey, I told you—we need that for bills!"

"It's my money," I hollered. "I should at least get to borrow it!"

The toilet flushed, and Ziggy came clumping out the bathroom door.

"Lid, Ziggy," Mom said.

"Oh, right, sorry," Ziggy said. He clumped back in the bathroom, slammed the lid with a loud thunk, clumped back out, and went down into the basement.

"Mom, if we win this contest, I'll give you all the money," I said, picking the flyer up off the table. "See? First prize is two thousand dollars! So could I *please* have fifty now?"

"Let me see that flyer," said Wendy, grabbing it away from me. "Hmmmm. Two thousand dollars. That's not exactly peanuts, Bev. Tim, can anybody enter this contest?"

"Geez, I don't know, Wendy," I said. "I guess anybody could enter. It's a free country supposenly." I gave Mom my soulful don't-you-love-me gaze. "*Moooommmm??*"

"Oh, all *right,*" Mom said, glancing nervously at her friends. "We're already so deep in debt, fifty dollars won't make any difference." She laughed a resigned little laugh.

"Thanks, Queen of All Moms," I gurgled.

"Tim, you go on downstairs now. And if you're going to listen to music, keep the volume down. You know how Mr. Miller next door complains."

26

"I hate the neighbors," I said. "Let's move!" and I ran back downstairs.

Four listless artists stared at me apathetically, waiting for direction.

"I got the entry fee!" I yelled.

"All right!" yelled Flipper. "DogBreath rides again!"

I strapped on my guitar and put on headphones.

"Okay, troops," I said. "We've got two weeks to get ready for this contest at Lewd Fingers'. 'Hell School.' Let's take it from the edge. Only we have to be quiet. Mom's still having a class."

"Okay. Quiet. Yeah," said Ziggy. Raising his drumsticks high over his head, he brought them down with a rhythmic crash on his toms.

"ROCK AND ROLLLLLL!! Ah-one, two, three, fah!"

Suddenly, there was my mom standing at the bottom of the stairs, arms folded, lips tight, toe tapping tensely. And, of course, green gook all over her face.

"All right," she said. "Ziggy. Todi. Flipper. I'll have to ask you to leave. Now."

"Mom," I hollered. "Not now! We're right in the middle of—"

"Everybody leave right now! Phoebe, you too, dear, I'm sorry."

Todi and Flipper hove big impatient sighs, grabbed their gear, and went stomping out the basement door without even saying good-bye.

Ziggy snatched his drumsticks and loped out after them, shooting me a look over his shoulder that spoke volumes of bad thoughts.

Phoebe picked up her PeeChee. "Good-bye, Mrs. Threlfall. Nice to meet you." She gave me a loopy look through her blue glasses and went up the basement stairs.

"Thank you, Phoebe," she said. And then my mother *really* scared me—she burst into tears. She just stood there on the basement steps, her shoulders heaving, and tears getting all down her green gook.

"I don't know what we're going to do, Timmy. I just don't know what we're going to do."

You ever have your mother cry on you? You could get really insecure from it.

Chapter Four

Couple of days later. It was I and Ziggy's regular day to take our awesome guitar lessons over in the University District with Doctor Killboy Powerhead. Ziggy tried to start Veronica, his trashed-out VW Beetle, but she wouldn't start due to being out of gas, so we rode bikes. Well, I rode my bike, Ziggy was riding his skateboard. Except Ziggy gets too worn out to swoof his board, due to the fact that he's very creative and always thinking a lot, plus he chain-smokes and hasn't got any wind power, so I pull him along beside me on my bike. At least it's downhill most of the way from my house to the University Bridge, which is how you get across the lake to the District.

Back a couple of years ago when I and Ziggy first found out that Wendy worked at the bridge control tower, I noticed that there was this big mailbox on the side of the bridge. It just said "University Bridge" on it. The mailbox, I discovered, has an ancient photo of Raquel Welch wearing a fur bikini from the movie *One*

Million Years B.C. pasted on the inside back wall of said mailbox. It is the single most awesome example of art photography ever of all time. She's standing there in front of some rocks, clad only in an extremely very low-cut furry bikini thing, with this cleavage. Her nostrils are flaring in defiance of something off camera. She's clutching a crude spear in one hand, squinting in the harsh prehistoric sunlight, and there's this kind of lion-colored shoulder-long hair that's kind of wild and free and blows in the wind. Rent the video. It's . . . I don't know . . . wow.

A while later, I got in the habit of writing about things that are weighing heavy on my mind—like Suzie Blethins—and mailing them to Ms. Welch, in the bridge mailbox. I don't know Ms. Welch in any way, and I don't have her address. I just feel like I'm mailing my letters to the universe, and somehow it makes me feel better just getting stuff off my chest. Like Suzie. Like the band. And all right, all right, my dadandhowImisshim. Some people mail letters to Santa Claus. I put mine in the bridge mailbox in hopes that the universe will write me back. Hasn't happened yet—but hope triumphs over experience.

Anyway, it was a beautiful day, the sun was shining, boats sailing, the waves waving, and I and Zig were working on a new song idea, based on my mom's affirmations: "My life is getting better and better."

"My life is getting better and bet-ter! oh
I love this girl, but I cannot get her, whoa
At least she ain't ignorin' me no more, no

Now she throws up on the flooring before me, oh
My life is getting better and bet-ter! Oh
Better and better and bet-ter."

So we came bombing onto the University Bridge, singing at the top of my lungs (Ziggy doesn't have much lung power). We decided to stop by and see if Wendy was working.

First I ran across in front of traffic to drop off my weekly letter to Ms. Raquel Welch.

Letter mailed, we bounded up the spiral stairs past homeless beggars drinking wine, to Wendy's "Rapunzel tower" as she calls it. Or I bounded up anyway. Ziggy kind of staggered.

We burst through the little door—kapow, ka-*channgg,* wham—and there was Wendy sitting with her brown UPS-style uniform on, listening to a Walkman, with headphones on, pounding on her control panel like a drum, not doing that great but really into it.

"America is addicted, America is addicted," she sang along with the tape.

Suddenly, we heard a bunch of honking down below, and bells clanging. Wendy just kept on flailing away.

"Whoa, lookee, Tim," Ziggy said, pointing to the lake. "There's a whole bunch of boats backed up waiting to get through the bridge. I don't think she can hear them!"

"Shall we wait and see how long it takes her to notice them/us?" I wondered aloud.

"She might not appreciate it, babe," said Zig.

Suddenly, Wendy's CB radio crackled to life. "Wendy, Wendy! This is Wally! What the heck are you doing up there?"

Wally Edgemont, Wendy's dopey boyfriend, was at that very moment calling from the CB radio on his fancy sailboat, the *Derby King,* down below in the lake.

"Hey, Wendy! Wendy," I shouted. I tapped her on the shoulder. Wendy whipped around, startled, pulling the earphones off her head. Raw-sounding rock music came wafting out of the earphones. "You got some customers!"

"Eeeeee! Don't sneak up on a gal thataway!" Suddenly, she noticed the marine traffic jam down below.

"Oh, my God!" she hollered. "All hands on deck!" Wendy jumped off her stool and waved out the window to the boats.

"Can I pull the lever, man?" Ziggy asked.

"Just let me just punch in the numbers first." She ran to the electronic console and started the traffic light program. "Give the horn a blast, Timmy!"

Bells started clanging on the bridge tower. As the traffic lights went to warning, the yellow-and-black-striped traffic barriers unfolded across the traffic lanes like a praying mantis grabbing a bug. The car traffic slowed to a stop; then the bridge deck split across the center and the twin halves slowly and majestically rose into the air like the jaws of a prehistoric swamp beast.

It's such a huge event, the bridge opening up—I always get crazy when it happens, like I want to fly—just jump off the ground like Superman and soar into the air with the birds. But for some stupid reason, people can't fly, so I have to be happy with sitting there, oscillating, watching the bridge go up. I'd always wished that some-day I could run out to the middle of the bridge when I heard the bells start to ding and grab on tight to the rail-ing, and when the bridge went up all vertical and vertig-inous, I'd soar up into space with it, dangling down, hanging on to that railing, laughing like a maniac. And then—I don't know—dive down, down, down, into the water.

So far I haven't had the chance.

Chapter Five

Back in real life; we watched the boats unjam themselves and proceed majestically through the channel. When they had all gone through, Wendy punched a bunch more buttons, Ziggy blasted the horn, the bridge floated down, the arms retracted, the light turned green, the traffic started flowing again, and life returned to what passes for normal around here.

"Thanks, you guys!" Wendy said. "I owe you one. This music is so loud, I couldn't hear the boats! I could lose my job if anyone reported me!"

"We won't report you," Ziggy said solemnly. "If you pay us one million dollars."

"How come you're listening to actual good music?" I asked.

Ziggy picked up the CD box. "You're playing 'Einstürzende Neubauten'? All right, Wen! Very excellent choice!"

"Oh, I was just being silly, I guess," she said. "I used

to play drums in the junior high school stage band. But my mother made me stop. She said it wasn't feminine. "

"Well, you didn't sound too terrible," said Ziggy. "But why don't you let a real man show you a few little technical points. First of all, paradiddle—"

Suddenly, a loud nasal voice interrupted us.

"Wendy, for cryin' out loud! Do ya wanna lose your job??" the voice reverbbed up the stairs. Wendy's gangly boyfriend came crashing up the stairs into the tower.

"Geez, I had to dock the *Derby King* and come running up here to make sure you were okay!" Wally stopped and stared at I and Ziggy in horror. "What's goin' on? Oh, my God!" he yelled. "Are you okay, Wendy? Have they hurt you?" He took a few steps toward us. "I'm warning you, you lay a finger on her, I'll blow you away! I'll call the police! I'll—"

"Wally, don't be a ding dong. This is Tim Threlfall, don't you remember? Bev's son? And his friend Ziggy. They may *look* dangerous, but basically they're harmless as long as you don't show fear."

Wally's eyes goggled back into his head, and his breathing calmed down. He looked closer at us. "Say, aren't you fellows in a punk band or something?"

"We are in a band," I said. "But punk was about twenty-five years ago, and although it was an undeniably brilliant and seminal period in music, it has served its purpose and gone its way. You might call us, if you absolutely need a label, industrial strength post-punk alternative retro rock," I explained.

Wally looked at me for a moment. "Uh-huh. You don't bite the heads off of chickens and bats and stuff, do you?" he asked, cleaning his glasses on his shirttail.

Wendy punched him on the arm, hard.

"Ow."

Suddenly a new voice echoed up the stairwell.

"Oh, my *God*, somebody get me a paper bag!! I'm hyperventilating!"

"Wendy, do you have to climb up all these stairs every day just to get to work?"

"Somebody get me an oxygen tent!"

At that moment, you'll never guess who came staggering into the by-now-crowded bridge tower. So I'll tell you. Jetta Prince, Mrs. Lewis, my music teacher, and my mother! Something very bizarre was obviously up.

Chapter Six

"Oh, God," sighed Ziggy. "Look. It's the Middle-Aged Spreads."

"Mom!" I said, elbowing Ziggy. "What are you doing here?"

"I need to sit down before I fall down," said Mrs. Lewis, pulling up a stool. "Wendy, do you climb up and down these stairs every day?"

"That's how she keeps her figure," said my mother.

"Oh, hi, Wally," said Jetta. "How are you? I haven't seen you since you won that fishing contest or whatever it was."

"It wasn't a *contest*, it was a *derby*. Do you want to see a picture?" And Wally had his wallet out before you could scream no! "See, this is me on the left, and the fish on the right."

"Wally, put that picture away, would you?" Wendy said.

"Oh, that's all right," said Jetta. "I think it's very interes—"

"*Now*, Wally," said Wendy.

"Well, you got us all here, Wendy. What's this all about?" Mrs. Lewis asked.

"Yes," said Jetta. "What's this big idea you said you have?"

Wendy shot a look at us and said, "Uh, why don't you guys run along?" Ladies never like to have guys around when they're talking about private lady stuff, did you notice.

"It isn't another bake sale, is it?" asked Mrs. Lewis.

"I hope it isn't another wet T-shirt contest, Wendy," said Jetta. "Larry—my attorney? I mean my husband? His partners almost fired him—all because I his wife participated in that stupid contest!"

"And I could have lost my teaching job," said Mrs. Lewis.

"Wow," I said. "Wet T-shirts? How come you never told *us* about this?"

"Tim, why aren't you at your guitar lesson?" said my mother. "You're not skipping, are you? I can't afford it as it is!"

"I'm going, I'm going," I said.

"Okay, honey. Be home in time for dinner," she said, patting my hair.

"Can Ziggy come over for dinner?" I asked meekly.

"Well, yes, if Ziggy would like to," Mom said doubtfully.

"What are you guys having?" Ziggy asked. "Macaroni and cheese again?"

"No, Siegmund, I thought tonight we would have Beanie Weenies and Jell-O mold salad. Doesn't that sound fun?" my mother said.

"I'm not into mold that much. Maybe some other time. Tim, come on, let's shove."

"You, too, Wally," Wendy said.

As we burst out onto the bridge, Ziggy called, "Come on, Comrade Tim. Doctor Killboy Powerhead awaits!"

So Ziggy and I booked on into the U District, heading for the mysterious lair of Doctor Killboy Powerhead—I on my trusty BMX bike, and Ziggy hanging on to my jacket, zooming alongside on his board. We came to the top of the Eleventh Avenue hill, a sharp forty-five degree drop into the District. We paused, poised at the top of the hill, waiting for the correct psychological moment to take the thrilling plunge down the vertiginous slope into the land of the Lotus Eaters.

"My life is getting better and bet-ter, oh!" sang Ziggy, and he swoofed to the top of the slope, then launched himself down the hill.

"Geronimo! Benihana!" I screamed, and sailed my bike forward and down. Ziggy, obviously inspired, launched a monster aerial assault, trying out Kareem's front side 360 degree late shove, Agah's nollie over the bike rack, and the one and only Julian Stranger's power flight over the whole catwalk in heavy traffic. However, close to the bottom, he had to brodie to miss an oncoming Honda Civic. He took a huge slam, bounced a few times, then lay still and bleeding on the sidewalk.

I screamed down the hill, "aaiieeeeeee," hurled my bike to the ground, crash! and ran and knelt beside Ziggy.

"Ziggy. Ziggy," I croaked. "Are you okay, man? You're all torn up!"

Ziggy sat up groggily. He looked at himself. He wasn't too bad, just all scraped and bleeding. "Hey, it's only skin, man. Where's my deck?"

I looked around and saw his skateboard lying in the gutter, the wheels still spinning, but all right.

"Here, climb on the back, Ziggy my love, and let us be off and away to Doctor Powerhead's lair."

Ziggy tucked his board under his arm, climbed up on the hub of my back bicycle tire, and away we went, bloody but unbowed, to our guitar Valhalla.

Chapter Seven

Doctor Killboy Powerhead, my guitar teacher and musical and spiritual adviser, owns and operates the University Zen Center and Transcendental Washeteria. He used to be the lead guitarist for fifteen years with the most famous Seattle trash band ever, Sacro Egoismo. People were absolutely transfixed by his brilliant and inspired guitar playing. Some said he was better than Hendrix. But just as he and his band were about to sign a multimillion dollar recording contract with Smart Punx Records, he received a mysterious message from the Great Beyond through his amplifier, that he should turn away from show business and devote his life to helping others through Eastern philosophy and cleanliness. So he left the band and opened the laundromat.

The Washeteria's in an old warehouse. Dusty light filters down through steel girders from the flyspecked skylights far above. The place looks like an airplane hangar and sounds like some preconscious echo chamber.

The first thing you notice when you walk in the door is this huge gold papier-mâché statue of the Buddha sitting on a platform in the back of the room, soaring almost two stories into the air, contemplating the unknowable, surrounded by clouds of incense.

At any given time there may be five or ten people quietly sitting and watching their clothes spin around and around in the washer or dryer, counting pop beads in time with each rotation, or chanting a mantra. There are no coin slots on any of the machines. Doctor Killboy believes in the honor system, and people are asked to pay only what they think is fair. At any time of the day, you might see Killboy walking along behind his kneeling students and customers, smacking them on the shoulders with his Zen slapstick if they've nodded off. Or he might be giving a power-chord lesson to some young striving guitarist or other, for which he charges quite a *lot* of money. His theory being that you won't appreciate it if you don't have to pay for it. "It" being whatever you really, really want in life.

"Laundry is a metaphor for life," the doctor was saying to a student as we walked in. "You can't hope to clean your karma if you can't get pesky stains out of a T-shirt. Awareness is the key."

"Geez, Sensei, I got more important things to think about than my laundry," said this scraggy-looking guy.

"Not true, oh Knucklehead," said the doctor. "In order to have a washday miracle, you must first pass through the valley of the washday blues. No pain, no Zen."

"But Sensei—" began the scraggy guy.

"Shut up and get busy or I'll boot your scrawny butt out of this dojo!" hollered the doctor, hitting the scraggy guy on the head with each word, just for emphasis.

"Excuse us, Doctor, we are here for our lesson," Ziggy ventured.

Doctor Powerhead whirled around and pierced us with a steely blue gaze, his shaved, tattooed skull gleaming dully in the gloom.

"And who the hell are you?" he snarled.

"We the hell are Timmy and Ziggy," I cried, and flung myself into his arms. Ziggy flung, too, and the three of us shared a rib-cracking embrace.

"And so you are, my little teenage bliss cookies!" he bellowed. "And you are me and I am you and we are THE WALRUS! Koo-koo ka joob." I gotta say, since Dad died, those Killboy hugs fill in a few gaps.

"Boy are we glad to see you, Doctor Killboy. Even gladder than usual, if such a thing is possible," said Ziggy.

"Our band, DogBreath, is going to compete in the contest at Lewd Fingers' club, and we've got to win. Absolutely. Unquestionably. We need your help big time."

"Come along, grasshoppers," the doctor intoned. We trotted along behind him, following him up an open flight of stairs to a loft behind the Buddha's head. "Timmy, take out your guitar, please. Ziggy, did you bring drumsticks today?"

We unpacked our instruments, and I plugged into his amp, as the doctor pulled up some zafu cushions and lit incense. Getting settled, he reached over to a picnic cooler and took out a can of beer, popped the top, chugged it, crumpled the can, tossed it over his shoulder into the trash, and opened another one. All in about ten seconds.

"Boys, take a seat," he directed. We sat cross-legged on zafus and faced the doctor. The doctor reached to one side and punched some buttons on an electric keyboard. Sequensized music poured out through the speakers—a kind of snaky caravan rhythm. You could just imagine riding on camels out in the desert, kind of rocking along toward a mirage or an oasis or an intertribal conflict. It had kind of a great backbeat, sort of like "96 Tears" by ? and The Mysterians.

The doctor picked up his own electric guitar and played an incredibly fast run that slithered into a state of suspended animation and kind of hung shimmering in the air, riding on the rhythm track. The doctor swayed side to side hypnotically as the music swelled on.

"Lydian mode, Timmy," he said to me. I began playing a simple modal scale in time to the music. Ziggy started up a lazy backbeat, while the doctor comped along with chords, and then would play a figure so fast you couldn't see his fingers.

"Doctor," said Ziggy. "Before we get too involved in our lesson, we want to ask your advice about this contest. See, it's really important that we win. Love is at stake, and honor, and survival."

"KEEP PLAYING," the doctor roared, and he tore off a guitar lick that sent pain and heartache stabbing through the air. We kept playing.

"Did you practice this week?" hollered Doctor Powerhead.

Ziggy mumbled, "Well, I meant to, but—"

"Get the 'buts' out of your life! Remember Reverend Ike's famous sermon! 'I meant to practice, but! I want to be a rock star, but! I want to win this contest, but!' Get the 'buts' out and get on with it!" said the doctor. "Only by practice, practice, practice does one advance. Sink yourself into the vortex of your music, let your body create your music, let your music speak through your body—your body is wiser than your mind, and more honest. The mind is an evil, devious monkey. The body is a shining angel of truth. Which is just the opposite of what most people think."

"Doctor," I said, staying with my scales, "there's a lot riding on this. Our career is stuck. We don't want to keep playing senior citizen dances at Seattle Center. It's humiliating."

"Humiliation teaches humility," said the doctor.

"And my mother is broke and we might lose our house and our car and our television," I said. "If we win this contest, I would give her the money."

"Small is beautiful, broke is good," said the doctor. "Saint Francis advised one and all to give away everything to the poor and to go on the road preaching the gospel."

"I don't think I have a calling," I explained.

"And," Ziggy chimed in, "Mister Tim is desperately, hideously in love with Suzie Blethins, a woman who will

never love him back unless he gets some status somehow in this world. Winning this contest would sure ele-
vate him in the eyes of our peers."

"Love is pain, love is illusion, love is blind, but the
neighbors ain't," said the doctor. "But! Love is all. So.
What song are you planning to play?"

"Well, we wrote a new song today called 'Hole in
the Ozone'," I said. "Do you want to hear it?" I started
strumming a dense, viscous chord change, and Ziggy
croaked out the lyrics.

"There's a hole in the ozone
Ultraviolet
There's a hole in the ozone
Ultraviolet . . ."

The doctor looked at us hard for a few seconds.
"Well," he began, "it's essentially a pile of mendacious
horseshit."

"Mendacious? Horseshit?" I hollered. "It's how I feel!
These are my true feelings!"

"Horseshit," said the doctor. "You don't care about
holes in the ozone. You care about love, life, sex, status,
power, fear, pain, death. Emotions. That's what other
people care about."

"Not at our school," said Ziggy. "They care about
football."

"They say they care about football. They care about
love and life and pain and fear and anger and sex," said

the doctor. "Give 'em what they want to hear and you'll win. Unless someone else gives them more and better."

"Well, how about 'Hell School'?" Ziggy asked me. "That's angry."

"Okay," I said. And we started to play and sing:

"They make you take these classes
That no one ever passes—
And all the teachers come from the Twilight Zone
Nah, nah, nah, nah nah!"

"Don't be sloppy!" hollered Doctor Powerhead. "Don't make mistakes! Don't try to play intellectually. Play from your heart, damn it! Play from your heart! Tim, have you figured out yet what is the sound of one hand clapping?"

I waved my hand back and forth in the air in front of my face. "Whoosh, whoosh," I said. "Is that right?"

"NO, NO, NO! Give me a break. Whoosh, whoosh, what are you, a wet washrag? HOW MANY WEEKS HAVE YOU BEEN WORKING ON THIS KOAN? Ziggy, what is the sound of one hand clapping? *What is the sound of one hand clapping?* WHAT IS THE SOUND OF ONE HAND CLAPPING? WHAT, WHAT, WHAT?"

The doctor reached over and shook Ziggy violently back and forth. Ziggy pulled his arm back and slapped Doctor Powerhead hard across the face with his open palm. Smack! Kapow! Suddenly, everything was silent. Ziggy and I sat, abruptly scared and shocked.

Doctor Powerhead sat, staring and glaring at Ziggy, not moving a muscle, his ice blue eyes burning laserlike, smoking holes through Ziggy's heart. Suddenly, he lurched toward Ziggy. Ziggy flinched back away from him. Doctor Powerhead grabbed Ziggy in a massive, violent embrace and lifted him off the ground.

"That's it! That's it! You've made a brilliant breakthrough! You've had a moment of true, deep understanding. You've seen the Abyss. You've met the Infinite! Whap! The sound of one hand clapping!" And he smacked Ziggy hard across the face. Then Ziggy smacked him across the face. Then he smacked Ziggy across the face. Then they started slapping each other real fast with both hands like the Three Stooges. Abruptly, a girl's voice broke in.

"Timmy? Ziggy? Is anybody up here?"

We turned to see Phoebe standing at the top of the stairs, looking particularly goony in a blue wool pleated skirt from some Catholic school, and a lime green fuzzy cardigan and penny loafers and no socks.

"I'm sorry—am I interrupting? Didn't you want me to meet you here?"

"Oh, yeah," said Ziggy, his cheeks red and chapped looking. "Doctor Powerhead, this is Phoebe Fortiere. She's singin' with us."

"How do you do, Doctor," Phoebe asked the doctor, and shook his hand. I cringed mentally. Powerhead held her hand a long time and looked into her eyes like he does with everybody, trying to figure out where she was on the great Wheel of Rebirth or something.

"You are Lilith, my little flower. You are Inanna, the Feminine Principle unchained. You have the purity of madness in your face." He turned to us. "This one is dangerous if unleashed, my sons. But if you harness her energy, she will catapult DogBreath to the stars."

"This is Phoebe you're talking about?" I asked.

Phoebe turned and smiled at me mysteriously as the doctor said, "This is the internal, *E*-ternal Phoebe I'm talking about," he said. "Now let's hear your song!"

Chapter Eight

I, Ziggy, and Phoebe left the Washeteria, practically on cloud nine.

"Yes," I hollered to the sky. "We're going to win the contest at Lewd Fingers'! We will become rich, famous, idolized! We cannot but succeed! We are glorious!"

"Extra-glorious," hiccuped Ziggy. "Soon, Suzie Blethins will be a willing slave to your small but distinct charisma!"

We leaped in the air to high-five each other. Ziggy crumpled as he landed, moaning in agony. His abrasions were still painful from his recent skateboard mishap. Phoebe quickly knelt on the sidewalk next to Ziggy.

"Oh, you're wounded," she cried. She yanked open her shoulder bag and pulled out some first aid supplies— iodine, cotton balls, something with Chinese writing on it—and started cleaning Ziggy's scratches. Ziggy's drumsticks and skateboard started rolling down the street.

"Save my stuff, man!" Ziggy cried.

I started hurtling down the street after the runaway skateboard. I managed to catch hold of it before it got too much escape momentum going. I was just starting to turn back up the street, when I heard a familiar, beloved voice speaking the words of a poem—

"Shall I compare thee to a summer's day?"

Standing staring into the window of Puss N' Books was Suzie Blethins, my beloved. She was with her friend Karen Olson, reading from a book that stood propped open in the display window. They both sighed.

"God, I hate poetry," said Suzie.

"Oh, me, too," said Karen. "It's so, like, you know."

"I *know*!" said Suzie. "I mean, why can't they just say what they mean, instead of all these metaphors and similes and junk."

I darted across the street through the oncoming traffic and recrossed the street a half block lower down. I ran into the Café Paradisö, which is this coffee shop with under-the-awning sidewalk seating behind a painted railing. I didn't have time to order anything, or any money, either, so I grabbed a half-full cup of cold coffee off an empty table, and ran out to the sidewalk seating area.

All the tables were full, except this one right next to the sidewalk railing where two long-haired, freaky-looking philosophy I guess grad students were talking really seriously heado à heado over stacks of books and papers. I jammed into a chair at their table, stashed the skateboard under the table, found a cigarette butt lying on the floor, borrowed their lighter, lit it, took a puff, coughed, choked, hacked, opened a copy of the *Rocket,* a Seattle music scene newspaper, and then, just as I had hoped and prayed, Suzie and Karen came strolling along the sidewalk right past my table.

"Yo, Suzie!" I said, I hoped nonchalantly. Suzie turned around, startled. Karen grabbed her arm, scared.

"Over here—it's me, Tim," I clarified.

"Oh, Tim. Hi," said Suzie. "I didn't know you hung out in the District."

"Yeah, I was just havin' a latte after my guitar lesson. You guys care to join me?"

Karen and Suzie started making code faces with their eyes, the way girls do. Karen kind of tilted her head at Suzie and was raising her eyebrows really high and pushing her face forward and bugging her eyes out.

Then Suzie rolled her eyes at Karen and looked away to the side and heaved a big sigh. Then she turned back and shrugged her shoulders. They both looked at me.

"Sure," said Suzie.

"Soooozeeeee," said Karen, giving Suzie an I-can't-believe-you're-doing-this look, but then she followed her.

I jumped up and grabbed two empty chairs from another table and jammed them next to the two philosophy guys at my table. I desperately needed another cigarette—nothing establishes an air of coolness like smoking. The grads had a pack of cigs on the table. I pretended to drop my newspaper, grabbed for it, and managed to sweep the cigarettes off the table onto the filthy floor.

"Oh, sorry, you guys," I mumbled, stooping down under the table to retrieve the pack, and slipping out about four of their cigs as I came out from under the table. I straightened up and lit my brand-new stolen Marlboro. Once again, I went into fits of coughing and choking. You have to remember not to inhale.

"Hey, kid," said this one grad. "We're trying to have a discussion here. Could you try to relax?"

"Oh, sure," I said. "Sorry."

The girls pushed through all these university students and fringies who crowded the tables, smoking, drinking espresso, and trying to impress each other with how sophisticated and world-weary and cool they all were.

I jumped up and said to the grad students, "Hey, do you mind if we pull this table over a few inches? The women can't get through."

The guys glared at me, yanked the table screeching across the cobbly cement floor toward them, glared at me, hunched in closer toward each other, and kept mumbling. One of the guys was doodling on graph paper.

Suzie slid into a chair. Karen squeezed into a chair.

"This is the coolest place," Suzie breathed. "What's the name of it?"

"Café Paradisö," I answered, inhaling deeply on my Marlboro. "They call it that because of that French film about—" Suddenly, I started choking and hacking again on my cigarette. I gasped and coughed like crazy.

"What's the matter, haven't you ever smoked before?" asked one of the grad students.

"Could you please not blow that smoke in my direction?" whined Karen. "I'm allergic to cigarettes. I really am, I get absolutely physically ill and have to go to the hospital—"

"Sorry." I coughed. "I think I'm getting a cold. Anyway, it's called the Café Paradisö after that French film *Café Paradisö* starring, oh, I don't know, Brigitte Bardot or Jean-Claude Van Damme or somebody. I saw it about a million times at the Grand Illusion."

The grad students were sneaking looks at me, snickering.

"Oh," said Suzie. She leaned closer to me. I could barely breathe from ecstasy.

"Do you attend foreign films? Tim, I didn't know you were so sophisticated!"

The grad students snickered again.

"Oh, I wouldn't call myself sophisticated. I just can't stand the crap that passes for Art in American culture."

"Well, I wish somebody would take me to a foreign film. My parents are hopeless."

"Well," I said, sighing, "maybe someone such as myself could escort you—"

The grad students were openly laughing.

"What's the matter with you guys?" I asked, belligerently I hoped.

"Oh, nothing." They chortled.

"Listen, Suzie," I said. "I have an even better idea. My band, you know, DogBreath, well, we are playing at this very hip, artistic event at Lewd Fingers' club next week."

"You're in a band?" Suzie said. "Oh, that is so cool!"

"Oh, horsepucky, *everybody's* in a band," said Karen, twirling her eyeballs around.

I jumped in quick before Karen could get on a roll.

"The press is going to be there and everything. I'd rea[l]
like it if you could come. It would mean a lot to me. I kno[w]
you appreciate art and music and poetry and everything."

"I don't know if my parents would let me go. The Dirt
Club has a really bad reputation," Suzie said.

The waitress slouched up to our table. She had grape
purple and bleached blond hair with dark roots showing, Frankenstein boots over ribbed tights, and a Swiss
army tank top, olive drab, with her black armpit hair
poking out from her armpits.

"Get you guys something?" She yawned.

"I'll have a Diet Sprite," said Karen.

"Diet Coke," said Suzie.

"Bring her a tall double mocha with 2 percent and a
shot of vanilla," I ordered the waitperson. To Suzie I said,
"I hope you like chocolate."

"Oh, chocolate. I would kill for anything chocolate."

"Diet Sprite," said Karen.

"Don't you want a mocha, Karen?" asked Suzie.

Karen wrinkled her nose. "I hate coffee. And if you
even say the word chocolate to me, I break out in these
big ugly pimples."

"Chocolate, chocolate, chocolate," I droned. Karen
glared.

"Diet Sprite," she repeated monotonously.

"Diet Sprite," said the waitress. "Ginchy." She moved
away through the crowd.

"So, you take guitar lessons?" asked Suzie.

"Oh, yeah," I said, drawing on my cigarette but not
really inhaling. "My life is music. I'm only in school

because I have to be. But you don't learn anything in school. Not really. You have to get out and live life to learn about life. They should teach life in school!"

"Yeah, like how to fill out income tax returns," said Karen.

"No, not that crap. I mean finding out what life's really about . . ."

The grad students were laughing again. The waitress came slouching back up to the table with the mocha and Sprite. She slammed them down on the table, threw down a bill, and said, "That'll be four ninety-seven."

I suddenly remembered I didn't have any money.

"Put it on my tab, would ya," I murmured.

The waitress jerked her thumb back at a tiny sign over the cash register inside. PLEASE PAY WHEN SERVED, it read, like the bottom line on an eye chart.

"Do you take credit cards?" I asked, flashing a MasterCard that belonged to my dad. It's expired, but it looks good.

"No credit cards, no checks," recited the waitress. "Cash only, please."

"Uh, just a minute—I have to run up the street. I think I left my wallet—"

"Hey, Tim, my man!" came a shout from the sidewalk. I jumped, and my arm swung in a big flinging circle. Mocha and Diet Sprite went toppling off the table onto Karen's and Suzie's laps. Karen and Suzie screamed.

I turned to see Ziggy and Phoebe standing out on the sidewalk looking at us. Phoebe was pushing my bicycle.

Ziggy had this sweater tied around his leg, but he looked better.

"Where you been? Where's my deck? We've been waitin' on you for about ten minutes," Ziggy said. "Our girlfriend here (he pointed at Phoebe) started to get worried."

"Ooohhhh, *sugar* beets, my skirt is ruined," Suzie groaned. She picked up the empty cup off her lap, held it upside down over the table, and shook out the remaining coffee. Big sloppy drops of coffee splashed over the books and papers belonging to the philosophy students.

"Hey, watch the books, would ya, jerk-face?" hollered the larger of the two guys. He snatched the cup away from Suzie and shook it over her head.

"Eeeeeeee!!!" screamed Suzie.

"Excuse me," I said, getting to my feet. "Uh, I don't think you should do that."

"Yeah, and what are you going to do about it, you pretentious little twink?" said the grad student.

"Well, I believe in nonviolence, but I can't tolerate hostility toward women," I said, trying to keep my voice from shaking.

"My, how politically correct," he said. He gave me a shove in the middle of my chest. I went crashing over backward, knocking over the table, my chair, and landing on this giant biker guy behind me, before I crumpled to the concrete floor.

"Tim Threlfall," hollered Suzie, jumping to her feet. "This shirt is 'dry-clean only.' You can pay to have it cleaned or else buy me a new one, and besides that I hate you!"

"Come on Suzie," said Karen. "Let's get out of here."

I scrambled to my feet, trying to maintain some shred of dignity.

"Are you okay, Tim?" asked Phoebe adenoidally from the sidewalk. "Here, let me help you." She reached over the railing and yanked on my arm, practically pulling it out of the socket.

Suzie and Karen came out of the front door and headed up the sidewalk, madly sponging off their clothes with Kleenex.

"Who's that?" I heard Suzie say, indicating Phoebe.

"Didn't you hear? That *thing* said she was Tim's *girl-friend*," sneered Karen.

"She looks about his level," said Suzie. "She's a real duh."

They disappeared up the street. I grabbed Zig's skateboard, climbed over the railing, and dropped onto the sidewalk.

"Let's get out of here," I said. I felt more depressed than even when my dad died.

"Hey, kid, are you going to pay for your order?" the waitress called.

"Do you have any cash, Ziggy?" I asked. Ziggy shook his head no.

"I'm tapped out," he said.

"Phoebe," I pleaded.

"Uh-uh," she said.

"I said, are you going to pay for your order?" the waitress persisted.

"No, I am not," I said. "We didn't get to drink our beverages because these tables are so rickety they won't even hold up a cup of coffee, so I don't see why I should pay for anything."

"*Tables* don't knock over drinks, *people* do," said the waitress. "You better wait right there," she said.

"No way, bébé," said Ziggy. "Come on, dudes! Let's split!" I grabbed my bicycle from Phoebe. I jumped in the saddle, Phoebe climbed on behind, Ziggy kick started his skateboard, and we screamed around the corner, across to Roosevelt, and back toward Montlake as fast as we could go. We had gotten almost two blocks, when a black-and-white police cruiser with its siren screaming and its cherry top flashing, pulled over. Two policepersons jumped out and trucked over to us.

"All right, all right, what you guys running from? A little robbery or something?" said the meanest-looking one, grabbing me roughly. I and Phoebe jumped off the bike. It crashed to the ground. "Hands against the car. Spread your legs. Don't even think about trying anything funny!"

And the policeperson ran her karate-hardened hands up and down my blameless body.

"This one's clean," she said to her partner.

"So're these two."

The policeperson spun me around hard.

"Okay. Let's see some ID."

Chapter Nine

Sergeant Ratched, this very muscular and mean-looking Caucasoid police sergeant person, parked herself in front of me, hands on her hips. Officer Waters, an athletic sort of Africanoid policeperson, came around the front of the cruiser, stuck her foot up on the fender, punched in numbers on a cellular telephone, and started talking into it. The police car radio belched out loud fragments of static and butcho voices.

"Let's see some ID," Sergeant Ratched repeated.

"We didn't do anything wrong," hollered Ziggy. "This is just another Fascist Amerika plot to curb the freedom of Today's Youth! Are you going to read us our rights? What was our crime, being Young While Running?"

"Yeah, that's right," said Sergeant Ratched. "Being Young While Running! Ha! Now lemme see some damn ID!" she repeated.

I and Phoebe pulled out our student cards. Ziggy, of course, didn't have any ID with him.

"We better take this one into the station," Ratched barked to Waters.

"No, he's with us," I attested. "His name's Siegmund Siegfried Jones and he goes to Dixy Lee Ray High School."

Officer Waters holstered her phone and came over and started patting us down again.

Just then, the waitress from the Café came down the street. "Those guys ran out on a bill. Four dollars and ninety-seven cents."

"Is that right?" asked Waters.

"No, it wasn't us, it was him," said Ziggy very helpfully, pushing his dreadlocks out of his eyes.

"Pond scum," I said.

"Officer," said Phoebe, "he wasn't trying to not pay—he forgot he didn't have any money when he ordered, and we didn't have any money, either—he was just going home to borrow some money from his mom."

"That's right," I said. "My wallet got stolen. And I didn't even get to drink any espresso—some jerk knocked our table over and it spilled. I was going to pay, I swear to God."

"Are you going to press charges for four dollars and ninety-seven cents?" said Sergeant Ratched to the waitress.

"Well, not if they pay up within twenty-four hours," said the waitress.

"Okay," said Ratched. She turned to us. "But I'm gonna have to turn you over to one of your parents or a responsible adult. Get in the cruiser. Throw the bike and the board in the trunk."

The three of us got in the backseat. Just as I got in after Ziggy and Phoebe, guess who should ride by in her mom's silver Jaguar XK8 convertible driven by her mom herself and see us getting in the cop cruiser? Right. Suzie and Karen. Brilliant.

Suzie pointed, Karen looked, and they both laughed hatefully as Mrs. Blethins drove away. Could it get any worse? I asked myself.

Officer Waters swung into the jump seat in front and immediately started talking on her cellular phone again. Sergeant Ratched looked back at us.

"Okay, whose house we goin' to?"

"Not mine," said Ziggy. "I don't have a house."

"Uh, I guess we could go to my house," said Phoebe. "Except I don't think anyone's home from work yet. My dad works nights and—"

"What about you, kid?" Ratched said.

"Oh, God. Okay, okay." I sighed. I told her the address, and Ratched gunned the car, punched on the flashing lights, and squealed out onto Roosevelt and headed across the University Bridge about a million miles an hour.

As we drove onto the bridge, rolling under the lofty, cloud-capped green metal arches of the trestle, we gave a halfhearted wave up to Wendy's control tower. On the canal below, we saw a bunch of ships backed up waiting to pass under the bridge, clanging bells and honking horns, and a bunch of cars backed up on both sides of the bridge.

"Hang on, you guys," hollered Ratched. "We're gonna cut through this mess."

Sergeant Ratched turned on the siren and gunned the engine. The white Chevy cruiser raced down the yellow dividing line of the street, past four lanes of backed-up traffic. Suddenly, we could see the praying mantis yellow barriers unfolding, the amber warning lights blinking, the bell dinging, and the bridge deck starting to split apart and rise in the air.

"Oh, my God," yelled Officer Waters. "They're raising the bridge! Hit the brakes, hit the brakes!"

"I can't—I'm going too fast," cried Ratched. "I'm gonna try to run it!"

"Oh, Lord, I can't look," cried Officer Waters, hiding her eyes.

"Good-bye, my friends," Ziggy yelped. "You'll never know how dear you both were to me."

"All right! Go for it!" Phoebe cheered.

Sergeant Ratched stomped the accelerator as the cruiser zoomed toward the center of the bridge. The two halves of the grated bridge deck, like giant Jurassic jaws, were steadily yawning open, higher and wider. Our cop limousine burst through the yellow barrier arms. We went sailing up in a graceful arc, and then suddenly, sickeningly, we were suspended in space for what felt like an eternity.

There are times, they say, when time stands still. This was one of those times. Like in a stop-action photo or an episode of the *Tales from the Crypt,* the car hung suspended between the two halves of the bridge deck. The lake surface twinkled and smirked far below us. My stomach lurched like I was on the Tilt-A-Whirl at the Fun Forest. Then, just like in a movie, the car gracefully arced forward, the wheels bounced down on the other side of the deck, the car shot down the slope, hit the flat, and zoomed down and out onto Eastlake Avenue. Motorists, waiting for the bridge to come back down, screamed, whistled, cheered, and gave power salutes out their car windows as the cruiser screamed past them.

"Wooooo-eee!" screamed Officer Waters. "That was some drivin', girl! Give me some skin," she hollered. She and Ratched slap-fived about ten times.

"You guys all right in the back?" Officer Waters asked us.

Ziggy had fainted dead away, poor guy. He's like that in a crisis.

Chapter Ten

A few minutes later we pulled up in front of my house. There were two other cars in the drive, cars I recognized as belonging to Mrs. Lewis and Wendy. The two policepersons jumped out of the side doors, and let us out of the backseat.

"Okay, let's go," said Sergeant Ratched.

"Just a minute, you guys," I said, climbing out the door. "I think my mom is having one of her Mary Kay classes or something. Could I just go in by myself, kind of quiet, and see what she's doing first?"

"Yeah, okay," said Officer Waters. "But don't take all night, okay? There are a thousand stories in the Naked City—"

"Yeah, okay," I said. "But one other thing, too—my mom's real vulnerable and conservative and quiet . . ."

"She really is," said Ziggy.

". . . and she gets upset, you know. So could you kind of take it easy on her?"

"We've had official law enforcement training in the handling of parents/guardians," averred Sergeant Ratched.

"Okay," I said. "Come on, you guys."

Phoebe climbed out and helped Ziggy, who was still feeling pretty shaky, to get out of the backseat.

I opened the front door and started down the hall to the living room archway. All of a sudden, bang, kapow, music blared out of the living room. At first it sounded like four radios playing four different stations at once. In a few more seconds, the sounds sorted themselves out:

"There is a house in New Orleans
They caaaaalllllllll the risin' sun. . . ."

Wendy's voice broke through.

"Jetta, you have to be meaner!"

"Well, this doesn't sound like much fun to me," came Jetta's whiny baby-doll voice. "All I know is, Larry will skin me alive if he ever finds out about this."

Completely weirded out, I sidled down the front hall and through the archway. The living room was a vibrating chaos. Diet pop cans and potato chip bags littered the coffee table. Wendy was pounding on the table with a rolled-up newspaper, kablam, kapow. My mom looked almost like she was trying to play air guitar, or something equally humiliating. Mrs. Lewis was strumming one of those cheesy autoharp dealies. And Jetta was squeezing a small accordion, trying to sing, I guess, folk music.

In a few seconds, the police would be coming in to talk to my mother—so of course, wouldn't you know, the way my life was going, Mom and her usually boring friends would have to suddenly go totally freaking demoniac on me. I closed my eyes for a second, hoping it was some kind of fluky hallucination or something. I opened my eyes again.

Nope. It was real, all right.

It was all too tediously, embarrassingly, horribly, actually real.

Chapter Eleven

I just stood there with my mouth hanging open. Nobody noticed me. Wendy looked at Jetta.

"It's just not working—it doesn't sound right."

"I don't know why you always pick on *me*," Jetta sighed.

"Okay, everybody—one more time!" Wendy commanded.

Her, Mrs. Lewis, and my mom started singing. Jetta just sat there.

"Sing, Jetta! Come on!" said Wendy.

Suddenly, my mom turned and noticed me.

"Tim! EEEEEK!"

I had nearly forgotten about the police outside. I'd never seen my mom and her friends behaving so—spontaneously, I don't know.

"What are you guys doing?" I asked.

"Nothing," said my mom.

"You act like you been doing the doob," I joked.

"What do you mean?"

"Smoking weed."

"Tim!"

"No!"

"We were practicing," explained Jetta.

"For a Mary Kay convention!" Mom added.

"Music to put makeup on by," said Mrs. Lewis.

"We better get home, gals, and practice everything!" said Jetta.

"Carol—don't forget to go down to the headquarters and sign us up," my mom said to Mrs. Lewis.

"Right. Bye! Bye, Tim, nice to see you!" said Mrs. Lewis as she zipped out the door.

Suddenly, she zipped back in, her eyes bugging out, Jetta and Wendy right behind her.

"Bev, there's pol*ice* at your front door!" she shrieked.

"What *now*?" my mom asked the ceiling.

I looked for somewhere to hide and gave up.

"Larry will skin me *alive*," cried Jetta. "Eeek!"

Jetta eeked because at that moment, Officers Ratched and Waters came sauntering down the front hall, bow-legged as a couple of cowpokes, pushing Ziggy and Phoebe in front of them.

"Which one a you's Ms. Threlfall?" asked Sergeant Ratched, showing her badge.

"I—I am," said my mom. "Is there—what seems to be the—"

"Ms. Threlfall, are you now or have you at any time ever been the legal parent or guardian of Timothy Benedetti Threlfall?"

"Benedetti? Cool! 'Ey, thatssa spicy meat-a ball! Arrivaderci Roma!" croaked Ziggy.

"Shut up, rag top!" I explained.

"Quieten up!" barked Officer Waters. "Who's the parent or guardian? You?" she asked Mrs. Lewis.

"I'm Tim's *mother*," Mom said. "If that's what you mean."

"She really is," Jetta chirped. "I swear. My husband's an attorney."

"My life is getting better and better my life is getting better and—Tim, what did you do?"

"I didn't do anything!" I yelped. "I'm innocent!"

"Ziggy, I blame you for this," Mom said.

"It wasn't me—it was Suzie Blethins," hiccuped Ziggy.

"Shut UP!" I hissed.

"He tried to pay—they wouldn't take a credit card," said Phoebe. "Really, he didn't do anything, Mrs. Threlfall."

"Call me Bev, Phoebe," said my mom.

"Okay, Mrs.—Bev."

"And where did you get a credit—"

"I'm these children's teacher, officer," said Mrs. Lewis. "If you need a character reference or anything— these are good kids, they really are. Nice. Law-abiding. Usually."

"Yeah, that's what they all say," sighed Officer Waters. "And then a tragedy like this occurs."

"I'm not even involved here," said Jetta. "Could I please leave?"

"Go right ahead on, Benedict Arnold," said Wendy. "Except you're riding with me."

"Officer, what is the charge?" said Mom.

"Well, we haven't formally charged the perp, here," said Ratched. "But he was attempting to flee the scene of the crime in order to evade payment of a debit he incurred at the Café Paradisö on University Way."

"Oh, Tim! No! Look, Officer, his father just died a few months ago—he's upset. Depressed. Hostile. He's usually . . . he used to be . . . well, I mean he's normally such a good kid—"

Ziggy staggered over to the BarcaLounger. "I gotta sit down. I'm still faint from flying over the—"

"You *best* keep quiet, kid—top secret official police business," growled Officer Waters out of the side of her mouth.

Ziggy grabbed the remote and turned on the TV.

"No TV-watching in the living room, Ziggy."

"Turn that off, kid!" snapped Waters.

"Yeah, right, can't ever do anything, sieg heil," mumbled Zig.

"How much—" my mom asked. "We don't have a lot of money—"

"The bill was four dollar ninety-seven cent," said Sergeant Ratched, sounding a lot like Robocop.

"I'll see he clears it up right away," said my mom. "If Nick was alive, none of this would—"

"Don't sweat it, Ms. Threlfall. Try to take care of that bill today. And you, kid—you were lucky this time. But I'll be keepin' an eye on you—if you pull a stunt like this again, you know you'll be spending a nighty-night in the slammer. Let's saddle up, Waters," said Sergeant Ratched. She and Waters turned to go.

"Oh, yeah, hey," asked Waters, turning back. "Who was that singing in here, anyway, before?"

"Why do you ask?" gasped Jetta. "Is singing against the law?"

"No way," said Waters. "Just curious."

"It was Jetta," said Wendy.

"Wendy! I swear—Larry's going to—"

"Girlfriend," said Waters to Jetta, "you *bad*. You got a singin' voice on you—mmmmm-mmnh!"

"Oh, my God, thank you very much I'm sure," whispered Jetta.

"You all be good now! Don't be breaking the law now! Ha, ha, ha, ha!" said Waters.

"Ha, ha, ha, ha, ha!" echoed Ratched. And they strode down the hall and out the door, hands on their gun holsters, keys jangling and clanking.

"Bye, Bev," said Wendy. "See you tomorrow!"

"Bye," said Mrs. Lewis. "Tim, try not to be too hard on your mother."

"Hey, can we get a ride from you guys?" Ziggy asked.

"Yeah, sure, come on," said Wendy.

"See ya, Benedetti!" croaked Ziggy, limping out the door, the sweater still tied around his injured leg.

"Bye, Tim," honked Phoebe.

"Bye, Bev! Bye!" chorused Jetta and Mrs. Lewis. They clattered out the door.

"What's wrong with them? Why did they leave so fast?" I asked.

"Just suddenly got tired, I guess. You know—old people," Mom said. "What happened in the café, honey?"

"Nothing," I said.

"Well, I guess we better drive over there and find out how much nothing it was. Who is Suzie Blethins?"

"Nobody."

"Is she your girlfriend?"

"I don't have a girlfriend."

"What about Phoebe?"

"Phoebe???!!!??%æëŸÿ$%##????"

"She's really sweet, Tim. A little awkward, but sweet."

"Mom, she's an incredible geek. She has a certain naive genius, but she's a geek."

"Be kind, Tim. That one's going to blossom. I think she might surprise you," Mom said.

"Right," I said.

Chapter Twelve

We pulled up in front of the café in a loading zone and left the car idling while Mom got her purse out.

"Let's see, it was four ninety-seven—I've got one, two dollar bills, and all these quarters, that makes two-twenty-five, fifty, seventy—oh, never mind, let's just run in and I'll dump all this on the counter—"

"No, way, Mom! Just give it to me and I'll—"

"No, I want these people to see that you have a normal, regular mother who loves you and cares about you."

She jumped out her side. Her hair was kind of rumpled up. She had this white T-shirt on that said WOMAN on it in plain black letters—like those generic products they used to have in stores—she decided she's a generic woman, which she thinks is so humorous.

I heaved a big sigh and got out my side and followed after her. Mom started up the steps to the café, then stumbled. She shrieked and fell down and all these people sitting on the veranda looked at her.

"Oh, hell, the heel of my shoe broke . . ."

"Mom, get up, everybody's looking at you—"

"Well, let them look. Go on, look everybody. A nice middle-aged lady just broke the heel off her shoe."

"You're not middle-aged, Mom, I wish you'd quit saying you're middle-aged."

She picked up the broken heel, limped into the café, and walked up to the counter where the girl in the horrible olive drab tank top, with her black armpit hair poking out and her purple hair, was standing.

"Hello, I'm Bev Threlfall, Tim's mother, how do you do," said Mom, a little too loud. "And this is my son, Timothy Threlfall." She stuck her hand out toward the waitress girl who stood there staring at her and not shaking her hand.

"We're here to settle Timmy's bill. Is the owner here?"

"No."

"Is the manager here?"

"No."

"Well, anyway, I believe the bill came to four ninety-seven?"

"Yeah."

"All right, here's one, two, oh, Tim—why don't you do the honors—"

She started rooting through her purse, pouring change into my hands. Three people lined up behind us at the cash register waiting to pay their bills. I started with the quarters.

"Uh, twenty-five, fifty, seventy-five, three dollars," I counted, feeling I'm sure I don't have to tell you completely ghastly in front of everybody.

"Here's some dimes, Timmy," Mom said, dumping them into my hand. She also dumped out the rest of her purse on the counter—used Kleenex, keys, lipstick, a small copy of *Daily Meditations for Women Who Do Too Much,* credit cards, scraps of paper.

"Three-ten, twenty, thirty, forty, fifty, sixty," I counted. Suddenly, a shriek rent the air.

"My contact!" Mom yelled. Her left contact lens is always slipping around to one side of her eye and then she goes insane. "Oh, damn. Excuse me, where's the bathroom?"

"Over there," said the waitress, "but—"

"Be right back," Mom said. "Timmy, finish paying the lady." Two more people lined up behind me, glaring at me.

I grabbed the nickels. I felt a muggy bead of sweat slither down my back. This process was seemingly without end.

"Three sixty-five, seventy, seventy-five, eighty, eighty-five, oh, here's another quarter that makes four-oh-five, okay, the rest of the nickels, four-ten, twenty, thirty, forty, forty-five, fifty. Here's some pennies—fifty-one, fifty-two, fifty-three, fifty-four, fifty-five, fifty-six, fifty-seven—that's all the money she's got in here. Just a minute—"

"Dear, waitress, can you take food stamps?" Mom came limping back from the bathroom. "I just realized I've got five dollars in food stamps—"

"No, we do not take food stamps."

"How much more do we need?" Mom asked the waitress.

"The total is four ninety-seven. You have very slowly and meticulously and painfully given me four fifty-seven. That leaves forty cents. Could you please like hurry up, okay? There's like about a million other people waiting to pay and get out of here."

My mom turned to the man behind us in line. He was one of the philosophy students, so you can imagine.

"Excuse me, I hate to ask, but could you possibly loan me forty cents? I'll pay you back right away—I'll mail it to you. We're just having a little cash-flow problem."

"Sure," the man said. He shifted his briefcase and books and reached into his pocket. "Here's forty cents." He kind of sniggered.

Mom took the money and gave it to me, then started rummaging through the stuff on the counter. She unfolded and smoothed a scrap of paper from the pile. She picked up a pencil and started to write. The point snapped off.

"Excuse me," she said to the waitress, "do you have a pen I could use? I'm going to get this nice man's address and telephone number."

The waitress heaved a huge sigh, pulled a pen from behind her ear, and flipped it to Mom.

Mom tried to scribble on the paper, but the pen wouldn't write. She set it back on the counter.

"Do you have a pen?" she asked the man who'd just loaned us the forty cents.

"Here!"

"Here!"

"Here!"

"Here!" chorused four people behind us in line, all handing her pens.

"It's okay, really," said the man. "You don't need to pay me back, I just need to take care of my bill and get out of here," said the man. "I'm TA-ing a logic section in five minutes."

"Well, I'm not a charity case, I just don't approve of taking money," said my mom.

"Okay," said the man, "next time you see a bum on the street, just give him forty cents for me—you can just pass it on."

"Oh, what a nice thought," said Mom. "Isn't that a lovely thought?" she asked the room in general. She turned to the waitress. "I only want you to know that Timmy's basically a very honest, trustworthy boy. He's just been going through a kind of a tough time lately. My husband died recently, and—"

"Mom," I hollered, "we have to go!"

"Oh, and by the way," Mom said to the waitress, "your outfit. Very interesting—"

"You *like* my *outfit?*" asked the waitress.

"No, I don't," said Mom. "Where do you do your shopping?"

"Mostly at Post Apocalypse," said the waitress.

"Mom, what do you wanna know that for?" I demanded.

"Maybe I am contemplating a beauty makeover, Mister Smart-Mouth."

Just then, a loud chorus of boos and hisses and cat-calls erupted in the café. I turned to see what the turmoil was all about. Out on the street, a tow truck from Lincoln Towing, with the big pink toe on top, had hitched up our double-parked Montego and was pulling it away down University Way. The café patrons, most of them looking like the kind of people who got their cars regularly towed, were shaking their fists at the tow truck driver, throwing food and paper cups at his truck. He cheerfully flipped everybody the bird out the window.

"Wait! Stop! Please! My car! Don't take my car!" my mom shrieked, hobbling out of the café as fast as she could go on one high heel.

Everybody was pointing and laughing and snickering and what not.

It came to me then, in a blinding flash, that I simply could no longer afford to be seen in public with my mom if I wanted to have any self-respect whatever.

Chapter Twelve-A
(because 13's bad luck)

"**I** never noticed how crappy this part of town looks in the daylight, Timmer! It's really rank!"

"Looks like your room, man."

"Looks like *your* room, you mean."

"Looks like *your* room, you mean."

We were on our way to the Dirt Club, navigating Veronica through a derelict old warehouse district. Dirty, decaying brick buildings. Dumpsters spilling over with heavily toxic trash, soggy with rain. Kinda like Veronica. Ziggy turned the wheel hard to avoid a couple of guys hunting for cigarette butts in the gutter.

"Grrrr! Rowf, rowf!" Howard, Ziggy's dog, stuck his head up out of the moon roof and barked at the guys.

"Be quiet, Howie boy. They ain't gonna hurt us."

Veronica didn't always have a moon roof—Ziggy created it with a blowtorch in metal shop. He took metal shop in the first place because he thought it was going to be about learning to play heavy metal music like Metallica and Black Sabbath. Boy was he surprised!

"Rowwfff! Rowf, rowwff!" Howie spotted a cat running down the alley and tried to scramble out the moon roof.

"Get back in here! Bad dog! Cough, cough," commanded Ziggy, yanking on Howard's punk-spiked dog collar.

Howard stands about five foot two at the shoulder, he's kind of dishwater blond, has terrible breath, and is nice but really dumb. We think he's a cross between an Irish Wolfhound and a horse. Every time Ziggy wants to drive anywhere, (on the rare occasions when he has gas money, or has siphoned some out of his uncle's car) he has to pretend he's going to take the bus, or walk, otherwise Howard demands to go along for the ride. And Howard is a very powerful and determined large dog.

A couple times, Ziggy tried some evasive tactics— like just before he was ready to drive somewhere, he'd get Howard all involved eating some dumpster burgers or something, then run out and drive away as fast as he could. Howard knew the sound of Veronica's engine, though, and twice he broke down the door of Ziggy's apartment and followed him.

For a while Ziggy tried sneaking out and rolling Veronica down the hill in neutral and compression starting her at the end of the block, but Howard jumped out of the window, cut himself on glass, and sprained his doggy ankle trying to get to the car. So Zig figured it was bigger than both of them.

"Do you actually know where we are or anything like that?" I asked.

"Dude, be real—how many times have we been here? Except not in the daytime?"

We passed the storefront of the Union Gospel Mission. Outside their doors lurk defeated, surly crowds of homeless guys and druggies and drunks and panhandlers and just generally speaking what Ziggy would call the disenfranchised, which is sort of the complete opposite of boozhy, plus some other types of guys that you mostly see their mug shots at the post office. It wasn't the kind of district where you'd expect to see anybody you know.

A couple of fry cooks taking a smoke break pointed at Veronica and busted out laughing in a rude way. True, she's a derelict, but she has character. Maroon fading to violet. Missing her rear fenders, engine hood, turn signals. Emergency brake doesn't work. Front fender tied on with twine. Bald tires. No ignition, so you have to hot wire her. A hula girl hanging from the broken stump where the rear view used to be. Seats covered avec dog hair, Pepsi, cassette tapes, cigarette burns, stuffing spilling out. The fabric on the ceiling dangles down in shreds like vines in some asphalt jungle.

Ziggy piloted Veronica through the mean streets as Howard and I rubbernecked. He took a sharp left, past a very disenfranchised assortment of gay bars and biker hangouts. Then he zoomed down a dark, cobble-stoned, broken-bottle-glittery alley.

"Stop! There it is, right there," I hollered.

Ziggy screeched over. A grease-stained wino lay asleep next to a flyblown garbage can.

"You stay here, Howard," Ziggy told the dog.

"Grrrfff," grumbled Howard. He gave Ziggy a big wet kiss.

"Yes, Howie Bowie Wowie, Howie stay heoh, otay? Dimmee a big doggie kissie, Howie." I practically dislocated my shoulder trying to push Howie out of the way so I could climb out of the car, interrupting their love scene.

We knocked on the club door. No answer. I tried the door. It was open. We peered in.

It was dark inside. We stepped cautiously in. A voice barked, "Close that door!"

Ziggy slammed the door. Blam, blackout. We were standing in pitch darkness. For a moment there was not a sound, not a breath, not the tick of a clock or the drip of a faucet, just the stillness of enormity. Then, bang, kapow: "All right, Weasel, bring up the blue lights!"

Out of the pitch dark, a stage suddenly sprang to view in front of us, flooded with hot pink lights. Standing in the middle of the stage was a balding guy with a greenish mohawk.

He stared up toward the control booth, a cigarette drooping from his mouth. He was kind of middle-aged, with a slightly fat stomach.

"That's him, man," hissed Ziggy in my ear.

"That's who?" I whispered back.

The pink lights got even brighter.

"No, bring up the *other* blues!" the guy hollered.

The pink lights suddenly went black, then came back on in a burst of amber, highlighting the sign on the stage curtain that read THE DIRT CLUB.

"That's Lewd Fingers," whispered Ziggy.

"He looks like he just got in from London," I said. "About twenty-five years ago."

"Blue, blue, blue, blue, blue!" screeched Lewd. "Come on, Weasel, work *with* the drug for criminy's sake!" Then he noticed us.

"Deliveries around back, little brothers."

Suddenly, the room was plunged into darkness again.

"Weasel!" we heard Lewd shriek, "I'm gonna kill you!"

Another shriek answered upstairs from the control booth. Footsteps came thudding past us and up a flight of stairs. We heard a chaotic symphony of things getting knocked over and broken, more shrieks, and other footsteps thudding downstairs. Suddenly, the regular overhead lights flicked on.

Lewd was nowhere to be seen.

"Where did he go?" I whispered to Ziggy.

To our right a door crashed open. Lewd stormed back into the room, pushing a very tall guy in front of him, whapping him on the shoulder blade with the flat of his hand.

"Go on, go on, get your butt outta here, Weasel! I've had it with you! My ninety-year-old grandmother is a better lighting guy than you are, man!"

Weasel loped along, hands in his pockets. He stood about six six, with shoulder length strawberry blond hair, a sweet smile, and green eyes that were focused somewhere very far away. As he came toward us, he smiled bashfully.

"Hey, Weasel," said Ziggy.

"Whoa," said Weasel. "Zig. H'lloo."

"I thought you were in Paris," said Ziggy.

"I *am* in Paris," said Weasel.

"Am-scray!" hollered Lewd.

"Catch you later, *mes amis*. Au revoir." Weasel shrugged out the door and disappeared.

Lewd headed back toward the stage. The long chain that went from his belt to his back pocket clinked and clanked as he walked.

"Ya want somethin' done right, ya gotta do it yourself."

I cleared my throat fairly loud.

Lewd threw a bored look back over his shoulder at us.

"We're not open yet, guys. Come back at 9:00 P.M. and get in line like everybody else."

"Okay," said Ziggy.

"Wait, hold on," I said.

Lewd heaved a little sigh, stopped, lit another cigarette, inhaled, let out a stream of smoke, and kind of whispered, "Yeah? What?"

"We're here to sign up for the band contest," I said. I dug in my pocket and pulled out the fifty dollars.

Lewd kind of shook his head, like we were asking him to do something really *unfair,* like his life was so *difficult* and all, but he went over to the stage and got a clipboard and pen.

"Okay, what's the name of the group?" Lewd asked, staring his blank blue stare, like Abaddon.

"DogBreath," I muttered.

"DogBreath," he said, scribbling the name down. "Too bad about that." He held out a roll of mints to me. "Certs? Ha! Just kiddin'! Arrr right. Oooo-kay. You got a manager or an agent?"

"No," said Ziggy. "We didn't know we were s'posed to!"

"Relax, relax, son. Lots easier for me if ya don't. Lots. Okay. Who's your leader? Your main guy?"

"I am," I and Ziggy both said at the same time.

I shot a very significant glance at Ziggy. "*I* am," I said. "I started the band and everything."

Ziggy didn't say anything, but looked very offended. We'd have to fight it out later. A thought occurred to me.

"Actually, if you must know, our real leader, our spiritual leader is Doctor Killboy Powerhead, originally of Sacro Eg—"

"You guys are working with the Great Powerhead? I'm not worthy, I'm not worthy!" Suddenly Lewd was looking at us more like we just might possibly be human beings. "Guy. With Powerhead behind you, look out man—you're either gonna be huge, or you're gonna crash and burn, career-wise. With Powerhead, there's no in between. Who'd you say was your front man?"

"Me," I said modestly.

"And you are . . ."

"I am what?" I asked.

"What. Is. Your. Name?" he explained crisply, tapping the clipboard with his pen like he had to catch the Concorde for the Continent.

"Uh—Moko," I improvised. You can't just have a regular name any more.

"Moko. Right. What's your actual legal name?" Lewd persisted.

"Tim Threlfall," I said.

"Threlfall, Threlfall, why does that name sound familiar?" Lewd asked himself as he wrote it down. "I don't know. Well, never mind. Okay. This is a very big contest. There's significant prize money, and a possibility of a recording contract for the winners. So have your act together as much as is humanly possible. Get here on time, have all your own equipment, have all your own band members, be of sound mind and body, at least enough to load in and load out, and play, and if you ain't ready to perform when we call you—zip zip, you're outta here."

"What time do we go on?" I asked.

"Next to the last slot—11:45 P.M. A great slot by the way. It's the traditional star-maker slot. And why am I giving you the star-maker slot, you may ask yourself? You humble little guys? Because, I answer, if Powerhead believes in you, *I* believe in you."

"Who's in the last slot, just curiously?" Ziggy asked.

"Let's see—what was their name . . ." he looked at the clipboard again. "The Angry Housewives. New band. No experience."

"Never heard of them," I said. Guy bands are always giving themselves girl names—Marilyn Manson. Jane's

Addiction. Barenaked Ladies. Alice in Chains. Et cetera, et cetera.

"Ha! Ha, ha, ha, ha, ha!" Lewd looked at me very piercingly, then suddenly exploded laughing.

"What, man?" asked Ziggy.

"Oh, nothin'." Lewd laughed. "I don't think you got much to worry about. Got your fifty bucks?"

I handed him the money.

"Uh, can I have a receipt?" I asked.

He gave me a blank stare, you know the one I mean, it's gotten very popular these days.

"A receipt??" he asked, like we were actually accusing him of stealing or something.

"Yeah, you know, a receipt, as in for the money," I said.

"A receipt," he said, shaking his head again. Whenever he shook his head, his tall green mohawk kind of waved in the breeze, just slightly out of synch with his head. "Hold out your hand," he said. I didn't.

"Hold out your hand, man," Ziggy urged. I did. Lewd grabbed it and wrote on my palm: "Received, $50.00. L. Fingers."

"There, that good enough for you?"

"Whoa," said Ziggy.

"Guess so. I'll go Xerox it."

"You do that. It'll be worth money someday."

Chapter Fourteen

With only four days left until the contest, DogBreath started practicing really, really, really serious. We chose "Hell School," "Toe Jamming," and our new greatest hit, "My Life Is Getting Better and Better." Geeky as Phoebe was, I was starting to have to admit that Ziggy was right bringing her on board. Her singing and general weirdness added that certain je ne sais quoi that makes a band unique.

On my own time I practiced guitar at home with my Eddie Van Halen *Learn How to Play Lead Guitar* video. My fingers were flying so fast even *I* was astounded, and I would just feel I was getting ever more brilliant on the guitar. But the minute I thought of the contest, my fingers would freeze.

On Doctor Powerhead day, when I went for my lesson, under the steely Zen stare of my mentor, my fingers suddenly acted like they were made of reinforced concrete and I couldn't hardly play a note. I don't have to tell you, this kind of problem could dead-end one's career as a rock star no matter how much musical genius was inside your brain.

I found a cassette tape of my mom's on the kitchen counter called "Conquering Stage Fright." She had every self-help tool known to civilization as we know it. I shoved it in the boom box on the kitchen counter, pushed the play button, and out came this lady's chirpy voice saying:

"First, imagine yourself some place in nature that is very calming. Perhaps a quiet woodland, or a clear, sparkling stream, or a sandy beach by the seashore. Imagine the blue sky, soft breezes, and the gentle sound of the water."

I tried the sandy beach, but I kept imagining getting sand in my shorts, and I kept seeing shark fins circling out in the water, so I switched to the clear, sparkling stream concept.

"Now, put yourself in your performance situation."

Mentally I had to transfer the stage of the Dirt Club to a site beside the clear, sparkling stream. That took concentration.

"Imagine now, that you perform perfectly, brilliantly. See the smiles on the faces of the audience as they sit, rapt, excited, thrilled by the genius of your talent."

So I imagined playing "Hell School," especially the guitar solo, but every time I tried to imagine it, I'd just imagine myself getting stage fright and everybody laughing at me and I'd seize up again.

"There now. Practice this visualization several times

a day, and soon you'll see that stage fright will soon be a thing of the past!" Click.

Mom was away every night working on some Mary Kay thing or other, so we'd just play until we heard her car come up the drive—sometimes midnight or later. But Tuesday night we were playing so loud, she surprised us. She told us we couldn't do band practice until my grades improved, and there was a bad fight.

Then to make matters worse, there was another monkey wrench in the works: Mr. Thompson. I quote from my letter to Raquel Welch for that week:

Tuesday.
Dear Raquel.
At school this morning I was standing in the hallway, outside the office door, talking to Ziggy, who was wearing a dress today, a kind of a baggy blue floral print layered over wool hiking socks and Frankenstein boots. We were arguing about the band contest Friday night.

"We can't practice at my place anymore," I said loudly. "My mom's completely against it—you know she'll tell Thompson if we do, and then everything will just be completely apocalyptic."

"Well, your place is the only place, Threlfall," said Ziggy. "We gotta practice. We don't practice, I for one am NOT PLAYING IN THE CONTEST FRIDAY NIGHT!!!"

"All right, all right, all right, call Todi and Flipper!"

"And Phoebe, don't forget—"

"Yeah, all right, and Phoebe, if you absolutely insist, and we'll meet at my place after school and we'll figure something out. Tell everybody to sneak around to the basement entrance and we'll practice for the band contest Friday night!"

The office door swung open, and Mr. Thompson, he of the Boys' Club Thompsons, stepped out from behind with a smug look on his face and said: "Do my ears deceive me, or do I hear talk of you boys playing in a band?"

"Your ears deceive you, Mr. Thompson," I and Ziggy both said at the same time.

"I think not, fellows. Step into my office."

We stepped into his office. We dropped down on the squirmy plastic torture couch, heaving sighs, which harmonized with the wheeze of the trapped air escaping the ancient Naugahyde.

"Mr. Threlfall, we have an agreement about your grades, your micro-goals, and your extracurricular activities."

"If this isn't about me, can I go?" droned Ziggy.

"We'll be getting to you in a moment, Jones. Tim— can you summarize our agreement for us?"

"I'm not supposed to play in a band until my grades get better," I droned.

"In a nutshell, yes." Thompson smirked. "You are on what we call scholastic probation. Now, until such time as you are released from probation, if I should hear of your playing anywhere at all, I will be compelled to consider that a violation of our agreement, and you will suffer the consequences."

"None of this is about me, is it?" rasped Ziggy. He was shifting, slouching, twitching, obviously desperate to get out of there.

"Not directly, no, Mr. Jones," replied Thompson, "except insofar as I consider you an accessory in Tim's delinquency. Now, since I am sure I heard you both discussing a possible 'gig' as I believe they are called, here is what I am prepared to do. Rather than suspend you right away, I am going to make an appointment for each of you with Marjorie Mamet, our excellent school psychologist. You may discuss with Ms. Mamet your difficulty in keeping agreements. You will each go separately. I think tomorrow forenoon would be a good time. And if I find that either of you has failed to keep his appointment, advertently or otherwise, it will be grounds for dismissal."

"Hip hip, hooray," droned Ziggy.

"And kindly remove the dress, Mr. Jones. You *know* my position on wearing inappropriate garments on the school premises."

"This is my lucky dress. I can't, man!"

"Oh, yes, you can, Mr. Jones. I am ordering you to remove the dress."

"You'll be sorry if you make me shed the threads, sirrah!"

"Being the Boys' Club counselor means never having to say you're sorry, Mr. Jones. Take it off."

"Man, you don't know, do you! You don't have clue one. This is not a *dress*. This is a statement. This is a declaration about freedom from Fascist bourgeois principles. I can wear whatever I want whenever I want, to show solidarity with men and women everywhere who have shed their life's blood for life, liberty, the pursuit of happiness, and freedom of apparel as guaranteed in the Constitution of the United States of America! I'm calling the ACLU. 'Oh, say, can you see, by the dawn's early light' . . ."

Ziggy's singing is not of the best, by most standards, as you may have gathered. He has a very high, gargly, shaky kind of strangly sound.

"Thank you for the deeply felt lecture on democracy, Mr. Jones. If and when the ACLU decides to advocate for the rights of transvestites, I will deal with it. Until such time, kindly remove that dress!"

Ziggy stood up and said, "Sure, man. Unzip me, Timmer?" I unzipped him, and he pulled his arms out of the dress sleeves. The dress fell down to the floor and there was Ziggy with totally nothing on except Doc Martens, lumberjack socks, nipple ring, and his Scorpio Rising tattoo.

Mr. Thompson rolled his eyes and heaved a weary sigh.

"You may put the dress back on, Ziggy."

The next forenoon, as Mr. Thompson had so graciously commanded, I reluctantly skipped Study Lab and reluctantly reported to the office of Marjorie Mamet, one of our two resident school psychologists. They call her Large Marge. I tried to think up a way I could get out of talking to her, but I knew that if I skipped it, Thompson would find some other way to torture me. I knocked on her door.

Ms. Mamet opened the door, looked at me like she wasn't sure what I was, and told me to come in. She was one of those people you don't want to walk right behind because you have to watch her rear end kind of kabloom-kablamming from side to side like it was two small manatees in a blue denim laundry bag jumping up and down on a trampoline.

She stopped right in front of a poster of these big daisies in primary colors, held out her hands, gave me a blinding smile, and said, "Well, let's have a big hug, Milo."

I don't know why she thought my name was Milo. Probably she had my file mixed up with Milo Monlux, a well-known psychotic eleventh grader. But I had an intuitive hunch that it was for the best. She threw her arms around me and pressed me to her bosom.

"We never hugged in our family, Milo. But my primal scream therapist got me started hugging people about five years ago. I tell you, the first time I hugged my cleaning lady we just cried and cried. I'm a big believer in hugs!"

Raquel, I feel I can tell you this, but no one else must know. I started to cry on the spot. Marge pretended not to notice.

"Okay, now, honey. Sit down anywhere you want. A lot of the kids like the beanbag chair."

I sat in the chair by the desk. She shoved the Kleenex toward me.

"Have a Kleenex, hon. Well, what's going on with Milo, today?" she asked. She fumbled around on her desktop and in a file drawer behind her. "Huh, I guess we don't have a file on you. Well, we'll just wing it."

She got out a yellow legal pad and pencil. I cried harder.

"Trouble at home?" she asked. I nodded.

"Girlfriend troubles?" she asked. I nodded.

"Trouble with your grades?" she asked. I nodded.

"Anxiety about your future?" she asked. I nodded.

"I miss anything?" she asked.

"Yeah, Dad died six months ago, we don't have any money, and my band's supposed to be in a very important band contest Friday night, and my entire life depends on winning that contest, but my mom won't let us practice, and if we play in the contest I'll get kicked out of school."

"Caught on the horns of the proverbial dilemma," observed Marge, scribbling away. "What do you think, realistically speaking, are your chances of winning the contest?"

"Crappy," I said.

"Hmmm, sounds like we have a self-esteem problem here," said Marjorie. She reached behind her and picked up a pad of newsprint, and a box of crayons off the corner of the desk. "Here's what we're going to do. We're going to take this nice paper, and these crayons, and I want you to write down all your positive qualities. Use just whatever colors you *feel* like. Use them all. See? Aren't these nice, vibrant colors?"

She lay the pad on the desk between us. I sat there stunned, staring dully at this sheet of paper.

"I can't think of a single thing," I said.

"Now, come on. I *know* you have a lot of wonderful

qualities." She boldly took charge. Reaching for the purple crayon, she scrawled in large script: *Milo is talented.*

I shrugged and shuffled and hunched in my chair.

"Now, come on, you know you're talented. What else?"

I thought of Ziggy and all I have to put up with from him. "I'm a loyal friend, I guess."

She took a chartreuse crayon and wrote: *Milo is a good friend.* "What else?"

I thought of Howie, the dog. "Well, I sorta like animals, I guess."

She took a very orange crayon and drew: *Milo is kind to animals.* "What else? Now, come on. You take a crayon. This is for you, you know. For your 'child within.'"

So I wrote a bunch of bogus qualities on the paper. I couldn't think of any of my own that I liked, so I wrote qualities I admire in my mother, in Suzie, Ziggy, and in Donaldine, the girl who cuts my hair once every nine months or so.

Then I dried up. Ran blammo out of qualities.

"I can't think of any more qualities. Not one."

Marjorie said: "I can think of one." She smiled this big smile, then winked at me. She wrote, in red: *Milo is handsome.* And she smiled some more. "Now, you go on, fill up the page." My mind went on meltdown for a few seconds, afraid Marge had the hots for me and was about to commit child abuse on my pale, slender self. But she merely kept smiling and said: "Qualities, qualities, go on now. If you can't think of some real ones, then just make 'em up! They'll be the ones your subconscious knows you need anyway."

I don't know how I thought up all these great qualities, but you better believe I scribbled about twenty magnificent attributes that I never knew I had before so I could like get the hell out of there *tout suite.*

When I finished filling up the page, Marge took some more crayons, drew a large, childish daisy at the bottom of the page, and drew some valentine hearts radiating off it.

"There. Now you take this home, and put it on your refrigerator, and every time you start feeling depressed, you go and look at this. You just repeat some of these things over to yourself. You have to stick with it, you know, you can't just do it once and then quit. But if you do this every day for thirty days, you'll start seeing some exciting, joyful changes in yourself! You're a great kid, yes you are, and everything's going to work out fine, believe you me!"

I got up to leave.

"Ah, ah, ah," Marge said, shaking her finger at me. "What are we forgetting? The most important thing of all?"

"I don't know—I forgot," I said.

Marge smiled an ecstatic smile, closed the distance between us, and gave me a great big huggy, huggy hug.

Then I took my butcher paper and headed the hell back to class.

Chapter Fifteen

As I crossed the crosswalk to the bus stop, still thinking about my counseling session, Suzie drove by with her mom in their silver Jaguar XK8 convertible. "Beep, beep!" Her mom honked at me to get out of the way. I stood watching the Jag recede into the distance.

"Hurry up, Threlfall, you're keeping everybody else waitin'!"

Jean, the bus driver, hollered at me through her megaphone. I trudged up the steps and into the bus.

"Bite me, Jean," I invited.

As I tromped past Jean, she reached out her black leather-gloved hand and grabbed my rolled-up butcher paper.

"What have we got here, our little crafts project?"

"Jean, give me that back," I hollered.

"Relax, relax, Threlfall." She unrolled the butcher paper, scanned it, then looked up at me through her mirrored shades and said, "Awwwwww. Idn't dat tweet!"

She stood up and held up the paper and showed it to everybody on the bus.

"Look, evvwybody, idn't dis tweet? Timmy has a crush on Milo! Looky here! Milo is talented! Milo is handsome! Milo is kind to animals! Whoooooeeee!"

I snatched the poster from her and stomped down the aisle, and flung myself into the first available seat, which happened to be beside Phoebe.

"Hi, Tib," she said.

"Don't talk to me, man," I growled.

Phoebe shrugged, nodded. She had on a yellow plastic headband with these infuriating little cloth flowers glued onto it. She smelled like roses, which I've always halfway liked.

She got out her notebook and pencil and started scribbling away. As her head tilted forward over the paper, her blond hair would kind of slide forward, too. It was kind of baby fine and kind of feathery on the ends like a baby duck or something and also smelled like roses. Every once in a while she'd stop, stick her pencil in her teeth, shove her hair out of her eyes, then scribble some more. Then she'd hum, then she'd write.

"Oh, yeah," I growled, "you're supposed to come over to band practice today after school. Except my mom isn't supposed to know about it."

She didn't look at me or anything. She just kind of nodded her head.

"Right after school," I said.

She nodded.

"Like don't even go home first, just get off the bus with me," I said.

She nodded.

"What are you writing?" I asked.

She didn't say anything, just shoved the paper in my face. I couldn't really read it, the writing was so tiny.

"A song?" I asked.

She nodded.

"What's the matter, aren't you talking to me, too?" I asked.

She wrote something on her paper, so small I could barely make it out. Finally I discerned that it said: "You said not to talk to you."

"Very droll," I said. "I didn't mean it literally. I'm just in an extremely dark mood."

"How cub?" she murmured, scribbling away. She reached in her cardigan pocket, pulled out a used tissue, and blew her nose.

"Do you always have to talk like that?" I asked, feeling kind of evil as I said it.

"Doh," she said. "Just by adedoids have bed idfected for aboud four bunths. I'b goig to get theb operaded od preddy sood."

"Oh," I said, feeling like a total jerk. "I just kind of like the way you sound when you talk, is all."

"Oh," she said, scribbling. Now I will write her in normal talk, though she kept talking through her nose.

"Poetry," I said. "How come you're writing that crap?" I asked.

"It isn't crap," she said. "That's why. We're reading it in Mrs. Cederberg's literature class."

I grabbed the notebook from her. I read the following:

Eating alone, I
Pass the salt to myself. Jan-
Uary twilight.

"That's a poem?" I asked.

"Haiku," she said. "It's a Japanese form adopted by the Beat Poets in the 1950s in America. Five, seven, five."

"What?"

"Syllables in each line: five, seven, five. Seventeen altogether."

"Oh, okay," I said. "Like this:

Oh, Phoebe, Phoebe,
Phoebe, you're the strangest, strange-
Est girl I know of.

Is that haiku?"

"Well, kind of. But it has to have a season word in it, and a moment of suprise, shock, or Zen realization at the end. Like the first part is kind of like a photograph, and the last part is the poet's mind doing something new to it."

"Okay," I said. "Here goes another one:

It's Groundhog's Day—I
Wander lonely as a cloud
A cloud of nerve gas."

Phoebe didn't say anything. In the silence I began to realize what a sarcastic jerk I can be.

"How come you like it so much?" I asked, trying to sound nicer. "Poetry and stuff, I mean?"

"How come you like, I don't know, Suzie Blethins so much?" she said quietly.

"I don't know, I just do," I said. "It doesn't make any sense. It's like I got possessed by some outside demonic force against my will."

"Same here," said Phoebe.

"You mean you and poetry?" I asked.

"Yeah." There was a moment's silence. "And me and you."

Oh, God. I figured I must have heard her wrong, and didn't say anything so I'd have time to think.

Suddenly the bus squealed to a shuddering halt.

"Threlfall, snap to, this is your stop, curfew must not ring tonight!" hollered Jean.

I just sat there, slightly numb.

"Come on, we gotta get off the bus," droned Phoebe. She grabbed my hand and hauled me up the aisle, past Jean and off the bus. As I passed Jean, she hollered, "Bye, sweetie! Give Milo a big sloppy kiss for me!"

Everybody on the bus giggled out loud, but I didn't care, I had bigger problems.

As we came through the back door into the kitchen, I heard my mom talking on the phone.

"Don't worry, Jetta, you'll do just fine, just fine."

The door slammed behind us as we came into the kitchen. Mom was leaning against the counter by the sink. At the sound of the door, she whirled around, looked at us, her eyes bugged out, and she started whispering into the phone.

"Gotta go, Jetta, he's back. Okay. Fine. Don't worry about Larry and the baby, everything will be fine. No, I'm excited, too. It'll be the most fun Mary Kay convention yet! Bye!"

Mom whirled around again. She seemed to have quite a lot of eye makeup on.

"Mom," I said, "you're wearing too much makeup."

"I think it looks nice," said Phoebe.

"Thank you, dear," said Mom. "It's just a new line of cosmetics from Mary Kay. It's a little young for me, I think, but it's always fun to try on something new."

Mom seemed like she was talking too fast and her tone was unusually cheerful. I noticed she was trying to hide something between her back and the counter.

"What you got there?" I asked.

"Oh, this? Oh, nothing," she said. "Well, gotta run."

"Where you going *now?*" I whined. "You haven't been home one single night this week."

"I haven't? Oh, sure I have."

"Except for Tuesday night blitzkrieg."

"Well, maybe you're right, I've been so busy, I can't keep track. We girls are just getting our skit ready for the Mary Kay convention."

"Couldn't you stay home once?" I asked.

"Not tonight, dear."

"Why not??" I hollered. "I'm lonely! There's no one to

take care of me! It's like I don't even have a mother any-more!"

My mother's mouth got a bit tight around the edges.

"Usually, Timmy, you can't wait to get away from me and out of this house!"

"Untrue! Only just when you act all weird and stuff!"

"Which according to you is most of the time."

"That's because you *do* act weird most of the time, and you're acting even weirder lately than ever!"

"Your mother has a life too, you know, young man. I wasn't put on this planet just to wait on you!"

"Oh, really? Well, what's for dinner?" I asked.

"Macaroni and cheese, Tim," Mom said.

"I've had macaroni and cheese every night this week," I said.

"That's because we're very broke right now and I can get macaroni and cheese four for a dollar on special at Safeway!"

"Well, couldn't you at least put some hot dogs in it?"

"Hot dogs? You want hot dogs? Oh, well, sure!" Her expression was suddenly grim. She stomped over to the fridge. She flung open the door, reached in, snatched out a frozen package of hot dogs. She whirled around, stomped over to me, and slammed the hot dogs down onto the counter next to me. "Hot dogs?" she said. "You want hot dogs? There!" (*slam*). "Hot Dogs!"

Outside, a car horn honked, three times.

Mom looked out the window.

"Oh, Carol's here to pick me up. Gotta run."

She grabbed the bag she'd been hiding, her wallet, and her keys and went to the door. "I'll be home late. Don't stay up. See you, Phoebe. Take care of my son. 'My life is getting better and better, my life is getting better and better—'"

And Mom ran out the door.

Just then, the phone rang.

I grabbed it before the answering machine could kick in.

"Threlfall's Mortuary. You stab 'em, we slab 'em," I said.

"Is Bev there?" said a man's voice.

Hmm, I wondered, maybe she's got a boyfriend. Maybe that's what this mystery is all about.

"Just a minute, I'll see if I can catch her," I said.

I dropped the phone on the counter and ran out the back door. Mrs. Lewis's car was just pulling out of the drive.

"Wait up," I yelled.

Mrs. Lewis rolled down her window, stuck her head out and yelled, "Sorry, we're late! Bye!"

I stood and stared. Mrs. Lewis's hair was all moussed, and she was wearing black raccoon-ring eyeliner. I ran back in the kitchen, where Phoebe stood waiting for me. I picked up the phone again.

"Sorry, man, she just split. Who's this?" I asked.

"Larry Prince," said the voice.

"Who?" I asked. I definitely didn't recognize this guy.

"Jetta Prince's husband," he said. "Who's this?"

"Tim," I said. "Whattya want?"

"Is Jetta there?" he said.

"Naw," I said.

"She said she was going to be there tonight," he said.

"Well, nobody is here tonight," I said. "I'm abandoned and all alone, as usual!"

"What do you mean? Jetta told me specifically that they are meeting at your house. My mother and baby Annette and I are here waiting for her to make dinner for us."

"Well, if she makes you dinner, save some for me. Those guys are all somewhere practicing for a makeup convention or something," I said.

"Yes, I know," said Larry. "They've been over at your place every night this week. Isn't it getting a little old?"

"Here? They haven't been here at all," I said.

"No, they've been there every night. Jetta said so," he said.

"No. They definitely haven't been here," I said.

"Then something very strange is going on," said Larry. "Jetta is a very truthful person, and she would never lie to me unless it was somehow for the greater good of her family," he said.

"Huh," I said.

And I hung up.

"Huh," I repeated to Phoebe, who just gazed at me through her blue plastic secretary glasses.

I heard the outside basement door crashing open and the clunk, clunk, clump of three pairs of Doc Martens going down the back way to the basement. The band was here.

There were only two days left until the big contest. DogBreath and me had a lot of hard work to do if we wanted to win two thousand dollars, a recording contract, fame, fortune, and, at least for me, Suzie Blethins's heart.

"Come on, Pheeb," I said. "It's show time."

Chapter Sixteen

"All right, stow it, mutants! First off, I'm Lewd Fingers, this is my club, and I want to thank KRAP radio for sponsoring this digable bash tonight! Wanna remind everybody that the three top winning bands here tonight move into the finals next week, and they get a chance to win the grand prize of four thousand Georges. And a recording contract with Chainsaw Records!"

Ziggy and I stood in the back entrance to the club, staring in nervous apprehension at the human chaos inside the Dirt Club. Out front, standing in the rain, the line of wanna-get-inners stretched down the alley and around the corner. Inside, the young, the hip, and the grungy mobbed every square corner of the floor. They hung from the mezzanine, and perched precariously on windowsills, stairwells, guitar amplifiers, and packing crates.

Inside, Lewd Fingers stood onstage, a microphone clutched in his hand, barely visible in all the smoke and fog that hung in the air above the rowdy, restless, noisy crowd.

The club was wall-to-wall people. Everybody was dressed in black—black shoes, black socks, black tights, black hats, black caps, black capes, black scarves, black sweaters, black pants, black shirts, black underwear, black T-shirts, black tank tops, black jewelry, black hair, black dresses, black belts, black skirts, black coats, black jackets, black leather, black garters, black sheets, black eye makeup, black fingernail polish.

The main flashes of bright color in the crowd came from people's hair—hair every color of the neon rainbow—LED green, throbbing pink, electric yellow, nuclear orange, violent violet, cherry cola red, ozone blue, and every combination known to the universe and several that aren't. The whole club throbbed and swayed and slithered and hummed with the excitement of Seattle's young, hip, alternative rock crowd.

"Couple of announcements before we move on to the next group. Would whosoever parked their orange Volkswagen Beetle, license plate 2SXY4U, in the ladies' can, please move it. It's too crowded in there as it is. Also, the police are lookin' for whoever gave their German shepherd a mohawk—this person or persons is in very deep doo-doo.

"Okay. The next group is one nervy ensemble. They've played YMCA youth dances, the Daughters of Poland car wash, and various functions around Rat City, oops, I mean White Center. Put your grubby little hands together for Beata Tomboy Sundown, singing their latest EP—'Love-Stained Hands.' Do it, guys!"

Lewd left the stage. Four Adonis-like guys with black leather jeans, no shirts, eye makeup, and really, really long hair came running out on the stage and grabbed their guitars. Their drummer was this girl, Beata Sundown, who looked like a sumo wrestler and had frizzy red hair that stood up all around her head about two feet high like Bozo the Clown holding a live electrical cable. She came stomping out onto the stage, power saluted the audience, and slung herself onto the stool of her drum kit. She opened her mouth and let out a screech that stood your hair on end, triple twirled her drumsticks in the air, then lit into her drum kit like hellfire broke loose. She lay down a ferocious, killer cut-time groove.

"Leeeeettttt's gooooooo!!!!!!"

The guys whammed into their guitars, cutting loose a storm of sound more shuddersome than a multimillion piano drop on Judgment Day at rush hour on the Friday of a three-day weekend in a force-ten hurricane. They lurched and loped around the stage, playing their guitars in all kinds of acrobatic positions. Their lead singer, Shane Fontaine, in between verses, would lean forward and start rotating his head real fast in a circle so that his long hair whipped around and around in a big whooshing blur. Then the other four guys would all start whipping their hair around and pretty soon you'd practically get sick to your stomach just watching them. It was like the dry cycle at Doctor Powerhead's Washeteria.

"Wow, Timmer," Ziggy whispered loudly, "maybe we need to get better hair."

"They need hair," I hissed back, "because they can't play or sing very well. We got talent on our side."

Nevertheless, the crowd was going psychotic. Everybody was moshing up and down in place, like a giant can of sardines wired up to a million volts. The whole club dance floor looked like a jack-in-the-box factory gone insane. The crowd screamed and howled.

The song volume and energy zoomed higher and higher. Suddenly Shane Fontaine threw down his guitar, jumped up and down on it a bunch, and bashed it into his amplifier till the feedback made your teeth hurt. Then he took a few steps toward the back of the stage, ran forward real fast, launched himself out over the heads of the crowd, and hurtled through the smoky atmosphere. Immediately, hundreds of pairs of hands shot into the air and grabbed for Shane's sweaty body and caught him high up and carried him around the dance floor. Then they lurched for the front of the stage and threw him back up on the wooden floor.

Beata screeched another time, the band all hit a final crashing series of chords, and the song, whatever it was, was over, but you couldn't tell because the crowd was so hysterical that you couldn't have heard a nuclear explosion in the next room.

"All right, all right, shut your cake holes," Lewd's voice rasped out over the microphone. "Beata has two more numbers to play while the next band, DogBreath, sets up. All right!!!" And Lewd left the stage.

*   *   *

"Come on," said Ziggy as the music started in again. "We gotta find Todi and Flipper and get our stuff loaded in. Let's go around back."

We pushed and wrestled our way through the tangle of people and back out the alley door. We spotted Flipper's maroon Camaro pickup, the bed stacked with amps and gear, parked next to a dumpster. The lads were just alighting from the truck.

"Hey, fellow men! Come on, get your rear in gear! We gotta set up immédiatemente!"

"Yeah, yeah, we're comin'. You guys all loaded in?"

"No, we just got here a few minutes ago ourselves," I said. "Where's Pheeb?"

"I don't know man, she's late."

Ziggy and I unloaded our stuff out of Veronica. Howard climbed out of the passenger seat and sat patiently on the curb, panting, while we unloaded our gear. Ziggy always needs a lot of help with his drum kit, being as he's so frail.

As we headed into the club, Howard started to cheerfully trot along behind us.

"Stay here! Stay here, Howie Bowie Wowie Doggy Man!" said Ziggy.

As we carried the last load of stuff away from Veronica toward the stage door entrance, Howard started barking at us.

"No, Howard, you big bad doggy man, you stay in the car. Okay? Stay in the car!"

Howard gave out a mournful little whistling whine and settled down into the passenger seat.

"Tim! Hi!"

I turned around. There was Suzie, Suzie, Suzie Blethins standing there. She looked like the pale sunrise in the east, the bloom on a new peony, a poignant autumn day. Except standing right next to her was her pal, Karen Olson, a vision in her maroon-and-white cheerleader outfit. What kind of a total dope wears their cheerleader outfit, without a trace of irony, to an alternative rock club?

"Tim, I'm here."

"You're here."

"Oh, Tim—" said Suzie.

"Oh, barf," said Karen.

"Oh, Tim, if I stand near the stage when you're playing, will you look at me?"

How could I look anywhere else? I wondered.

"Threlfall, we're up in about one second!" Flipper was standing at the door, motioning for me to go inside.

"I'll be right there," I croaked.

Suzie stepped close to me, put her hand on my cheek and softly kissed me on the lips, a chaste, virtuous kiss of purest silver fire.

"Win the contest, Timmy," she breathed, looking deep in my eyes. "Win it for me." She kissed me again. This time her little tongue darted through my lips, a million magic words right on the tip of it.

"I—I will," I said. My mind was lurching and churning like the spin cycle in one of Doctor Powerhead's heavy-duty large-load washing machines. The last time I had seen Suzie, in the hall at school, she'd been completely violent toward me. What could account for this amazing transformation? I'd have to think it over later, when my heart quit pounding and my forehead quit exuding ice-cold perspiration.

Suddenly, from inside, Lewd's voice boomed out over the PA system.

"All right, let's hear it for Beata Tomboy Sundown! A totally awesome gruppo! All riiiiiight! Next up, we have another truly cutting edge, musically deconstructo group of visionary madmen—you've seen them at the senior citizens' dance at the Food Circus—next, you'll be seeing them on the cover of *Spin*—let's give a big Dirt Club howl for—DogBreath!!!"

As I sat there staring at Suzie, suddenly, a familiar riff assaulted my ears—DogBreath was onstage and playing without me.

"You're on, dweeb-o," said Karen laconically.

"Timmy, you're on," said Suzie. "Merde!"

"I'm on! Sugar beets!" Or words to that effect. I raced in through the stage door, took the back steps up on to the stage, ran out onto the stage, and suddenly stopped cold. Out there in the dark there were about a million people, and every one of them looking straight at me.

Caution: Simile Crossing (courtesy Mrs. Cederberg)—the audience suddenly looked to me like a huge, hungry animal, lurking and shifting out there in the dark, licking its lips, saliva dripping from its razor-sharp fangs. That dark, demoniac, many-headed beast in the twilight beyond the stage wanted to grind us up in its pitiless jaws, and swallow us down into the burning black void of its humongous gastrointestinal tract, like so much boysenberry yogurt. In an instant, my blood turned to ice-cold Jell-O. Ziggy, Flipper, and Todi were churning out the sledgehammer intro groove to "Hell School."

"Grab your ax, Timmer! Start rockin'! Start singin'! This is it!" rasped Ziggy.

I looked around for Phoebe. She was nowhere in sight. This was bad, bad, bad. We'd designed our whole set with her backup vocals in mind. We were in doo-doo up to our eyebrows.

My guitar leaned against a monitor at the side of the stage. I picked it up, feeling like a sleepwalker. I strapped it on. I took a raggedy breath, stood up straight, and lurched up to my microphone. I felt a single drop of turgid sweat slide sluggishly out of my armpit and down my ribs.

For some insane reason I thought of my dad, the Christmas he bought me that Stratocaster—when he wasn't doing all that well financially. He looked at me with his kind, crookedy smile, patted my cheek and said, "Maybe you'll be a star someday and support us all in our old age! I love ya, kid." Did I remember to thank him?

I snapped back to. The crowd was still there, still staring. I thought, I will start out with a guitar solo. That'll get me going. My hand was like a chunk of cement. My fingers wouldn't move.

"Sing, Timmer! Do something, man!"

"I should of stayed quit when I quit," growled Todi. "We're gonna be massacreed."

I took another raggedier breath, opened my mouth, and tried to start singing.

"They make you take these classes,"

My voice sounded choky and wheezy.

"That no one ever passes,
And all the teachers come from the Twilight Zone."

Flipper, Todi, and Ziggy all chimed in on—

"Nah, nah, nah, nah nah!"

My voice was starting to sound a little more confident. A movement caught my eye near the edge of the stage. It was Suzie, smiling up at me.

"They make you take hot showers,
And read and write for hours . . ."

And then, as I sang the next line, out of the corner of my ear I heard a familiar, adenoidally strange girl's voice chime in with mine:

"First they rip your flesh, and then they
Eat your bones!"

I glanced over at the other mike, where Ziggy had been. Standing there in a gauzy blue floor-length prom dress about four decades old, was Phoebe. She was still wearing her pale blue plastic secretary glasses. On her head she wore a little fake diamond tiara. In a split second of delirium, it registered on my cerebellum that she had curled her hair or something. In another split second, I started singing the first chorus, along with Phoebe and the guys:

"Hell School,
Lord, get me outta here
Hell School,
No wearin' leather here
Hell School—
It ain't pretty!"

The audience was dead quiet. If it hadn't been for us playing, you could have heard a paramecium sneeze. Suddenly, I was sweating, not just a little drop, but a great big flash flood.

"Oh, God, they hate us! They hate us!" moaned Flipper. "We're dead meat!"

I looked down to where Suzie stood. She was glaring at Phoebe like she wanted to disintegrate her into the Dust of the Vampires or something. There was nothing to do but go on:

"I don't wanna go
Mama, don't make me go
Mama, please,
Mama, please,

Mama, nooooooo!!
Hell School"

By the time the second chorus came around, Phoebe was really in her element, wailing away on her non-harmony singing, way up somewhere in the ozone.

We launched into the second chorus:

"Hell School,
Lord, get me outta here
Hell School,
No wearin' leather here
Hell School—
It ain't pretty!"

I launched into Doctor Killboy Powerhead heavy metal guitar solo number five—the Shrieking Feedback Cozmic Despair solo. I'd practiced it so many thousands of times, it was as automatic as breathing. I ripped it. I shredded it. I felt godlike, power lord, king of the global village. I did the splits, I dropped to my knees, I played on my back, I played over my head. The rest of the band was slamming away in a ferocious groove. It was a magic moment in music history.

Then, gradually, through the edge of my peripheral awareness, I heard laughing in the audience. What was so funny? We were playing some very heavy and power-ful music, not the least bit like stand-up comedy. I heard Ziggy's voice behind me.

"Howard, get off the stage! Howard! Howard! No!"

I turned around. There was Howard the Giant Dog standing upright with his front paws on Ziggy's shoulders, licking Ziggy all over his face. Ziggy was pushing him away, trying to keep on playing his drums. Finally Howard dropped back down to his front feet and came trotting over toward me, an affectionate gleam in his crazed brown eyes.

"No, Howard! Go away! Ziggy, call him back!"

"Howard, get back here!" called Ziggy. It didn't do one ounce of good, Howard just kept galloping toward me, a joyous K-9 grin all over his shaggy dogiognomy.

Howard came loping up and barked.

"Rowf, rowf, rowf, rowf, rowf!" he said.

I turned my shoulder to him, I tried to shove him away with my foot. He reared up, taller than me, put his feet on my shoulders and started licking me, doggy saliva splattering everywhere. I squinched my eyes shut and kept trying to push him away, but when Howard doesn't want to go, you can't push him anywhere.

"Keep playin', keep playin', you guys!" hollered Ziggy. "Here, Phoebe, play the drums! I'll distract 'em!"

Ziggy shoved his drumsticks into Phoebe's hand, and came running downstage and grabbed the microphone. Todi and Flipper kept playing the rhythm section, but I could see in Flipper's face that he was way pissed off, I mean way, *way* pissed off. Howard was still licking me. Where before I was drenched with sweat, now I was drenched with dog spit. It's a good thing their mouths are cleaner than ours.

Ziggy started weaving back and forth behind the microphone like a snake charmer's cobra, wailing away, *"Hell school, hell school, hell school—"*

The audience was laughing hysterically by this point.

Ziggy turned to us and said in his best Michael Jackson voice, "Keep me covered, men—I'm goin' in!"

He hiccuped out with one last, *"It ain't pretty!"*

Then he raced to the back of the stage, aimed himself toward the audience, got a running start, and launched himself off the front of the stage and out over the mosh pit.

There are times they say when time stands still. This was one of those times. Like in a stop-action photo or an episode of the *Tales from the Crypt,* Ziggy hung suspended between the stage and the crowd. The moshers twinkled and smirked far below. My stomach lurched like I was on the Tilt-A-Whirl at the Fun Forest. Then, just like in a movie, Ziggy gracefully arced forward, bounced off Beata Sundown, tumbled down on the mosh pit floor—bang, kapow—and lay still.

The people always catch the singer when he jumps out over the mosh pit. They always catch him and carry him around and then push him along over their heads back to the stage. Always. They always do that. They always do.

But nobody caught Ziggy. That's how popular Dog-Breath was.

Chapter Seventeen

"**C**omin' up next, we've got the last group of the evening—a totally rad, and way cool new band, the Angry Housewives! We got Brillo on the keyboards, Charmin on percussion, check out 2000 Flushes on guitar, and Numzit with the lead vocals!"

Lewd stood center stage, peering out into the rowdy, angry crowd.

Phoebe, Ziggy, and I were in back of the stage. Ziggy was slumped on a packing crate while I tried wrapping his wrist with an Ace bandage from the club's first aid kit. Phoebe, a weird wonky vision in her blue prom dress, rubbed Zig's bony shoulders.

"The Angry Housewives!" Lewd repeated from the front of the stage. I looked over. Four girls carrying their instruments walked cautiously past us and up the back steps to the stage. From where we sat, in the dim light, we couldn't make them out too well—they all had wild, tangled hair, very heavy makeup, and a truly amazing assortment of clothing.

"Do I look as stupid as I feel?" I heard the BBW* one say, as she carried her electric keyboard past.

"No, but *I* do," said another one, dressed in a heavy-duty black plastic garbage sack covered with Mr. Yuk stickers and carrying an electric guitar.

"*This* sure helps!" said a third, taking a long swig out of a bottle of something. She was wearing a tight, short leopard-print dress, high-heeled boots, dark red lipstick smeared around her mouth, and a necklace made out of baby-doll heads and teething rings. She seemed to be carrying a large sack of groceries in her free arm.

"She's smashed!" said the first one.

"Just leave her alone, she'll be all right," said the fourth, who had a roll of toilet paper sitting on top of her head, with her long tawny ponytail sticking out through the top.

Ziggy looked at Phoebe and me. "Well, the consolation prize is—that chick band there can't help but be way worse than we were."

"No way could anybody possibly be worse than we were," I said.

Lewd came back to the rear of the stage and hissed at the first girl, "All right! You girls ready? Let's go!"

The girl with the wine bottle lurched, staggered, and nearly went back down the stairs.

"Come *on,* let's *go!*" Lewd repeated.

A few scattered boos erupted from the restless crowd. Several people filed out the front door, bored. Lewd trotted

*For big beautiful woman

over to the guitar player and hissed, "Come on, come on, gals, let's get this turkey in the oven!"

Lewd went up to the microphone once more and announced, "Okay, I think they're just about ready! Once again, let's give a big, fat Dirt Club welcome to the Angry Housewives!"

The guitarist turned to the drummer and counted off, a little slurrishly, "Three, two, one, zhero!"

The band started to play. Klunk, ka-thunk. They sounded terrible. The guitar chords were basic and raw. The drumming wasn't much better. The electric keyboard sounded like a cheap toy. Which in fact it was. The lead singer just stood there, swigging off her wine bottle.

The crowd started to boo loudly.

"Boooo! Get them off the stage!"

There was a clatter and a clunk. A crumpled soda can, thrown from the crowd, skittered across the stage.

The lead singer spun around, grabbed the mike, and hollered at the crowd: "All right, you little babies! Ah-ONE, TWO, THREE, FOUR!"

Their band cranked into a very basic, throbbing, three-chord power groove.

The singer, the one Lewd had said was called Numzit, clung on to the microphone, lurching a little, trying to get her balance. She sang, kind of hesitantly:

"Where do you think you're going? (nyah)
Get back in here, you toadstool! (nyah)
You gotta eat your breakfast—(nyah)
Before you go to high school—(nyah)"

She picked up some steam. Her voice began to swoop and soar, going from way down deep in the alto subbasement way up to a soprano that almost only dogs and bats could hear:

"You think I am your slave?
You think I am your servant?
I fixed your favorite cereal
But you do not deserve it!!"

At this point, Numzit snatched the microphone out of the stand and started lurching toward the edge of the stage. The rest of the band was really cooking, really cranking out this postindustrial power rock that was raw and throbbing and made you want to jump up and celebrate life in all its pulsating squalor. Ziggy, Phoebe, and I sat transfixed in wonderment, staring at this awesome group from our backstage vantage. The singer lurched down front.

"Eat your $%@@@!!!&& cornflakes (uh oh, uh oh!)*
Or Mommy will get mad!
Eat your $%@@@!!!&& cornflakes (uh oh, uh oh!)*
Or I'll go and get your dad!"

Ziggy looked at me in disbelief. "Eat your $%@@@ !!!*&& cornflakes?? Give me a buh-rake!"

And now Numzit had begun to hit her stride, was really on a roll, really unstoppable, really one with her material, kind of a madwoman on a tear, who forgot to take her lithium:

"You better eat your cornflakes!
I'm losin' patience, honey!
You better eat your cornflakes
That stuff costs a lotta money!
Don't leave 'em in the bowl now
They'll get soggy, for gosh sake!
For the last time I'm tellin' you—
Eat your $%@@@!!!&& cornflakes!*
Eat your $%@@@!!!&& cornflakes*
Do what Mommy tells you!
(Shriek, shriek)
Or Mommy will get mad!
Eat your $%@@@!!!&& cornflakes*
(Shriek, shriek)
Or I'll go and get your dad!"

Numzit ran over to the side of the stage and grabbed a great big open box of cornflakes out of the grocery bag. She started ranting and raving at the audience—"If you're late for school, I'm not gonna write you an excuse!"—and grabbing huge handfuls of cornflakes and tossing them out into the crowd, hurling the stuff over the heads of the surging, cheering crowd. With every new handful of cornflakes that went flying through the air, cheers and roars and howls went up from the crowd. The kids in the mosh pit were jumping up and down like human pogo sticks, waving their hands in the air and reaching up for the singer like she was the pope or Celine Dion or something. It was actually kind of scary. The singer ran back and forth across the front of the stage, hurling cornflakes, shrieking:

"Chew every bite thirty-six damn times!
Grind 'em or you're grounded!
Eat 'em or wear 'em!"

Numzit lobbed the empty cereal box out into the crowd. She reached back behind her into the grocery bag and came up with a carton of milk. She ripped it open with her long, clawlike nails. She held it high over the heads of the people in the mosh pit, waving the carton back and forth in the air. The other women in the band were chanting over the clanging, pounding music: *"Eat 'em, eat 'em, eat 'em, eat 'em!"*

The singer tipped the milk carton to her lips, took a deep glug of milk, then grabbed the carton by the bottom and started whipping the carton back and forth, spraying the entire carton of milk in a white-like-stars-at-night cascade over the heads of the ecstatic crowd!

"Eat 'em, eat 'em, eat 'em, eat 'em, eat 'em!"

The crowd chanted along with the band. On the last giant, reverbbing, crashing chord of music, the singer screamed out one last "EAT 'EM!!!!" and then stood there, frozen, hypnotized.

The crowd erupted in a screaming, roaring frenzy, jumping up and down, rushing the stage, trying to climb up to get at the singer and her band.

Lewd ran out on stage. A couple of bouncers followed close behind, growling and threatening the wild crowd to keep them from crushing the stage. Lewd grabbed the microphone, his tall green mohawk waving like cornstalks in a summer squall. He took a deep breath, opened an envelope, read it, and hollered into the microphone:

"Shut up down there! Quiet! I said shut up! The judges have made their decision!"

The crowd subsided somewhat. Lewd held up the paper.

"First runner-up, Beata Tomboy Sundown! Second runner-up, Swollen Monkeez! Third runner-up, Payperkutz! And the winner is, drum roll, cymbal crash—the Angry Housewives! See you all here next week for the big $4,000 play-off!"

The crowd shrieked like forty thousand noon whistles in the third circle of hell.

Numzit collapsed to the floor in a dead faint.

Ziggy turned and gave me and Phoebe a look of the purest, deepest, disgust.

"And I said they were gonna at least be worse than us. Boy, am I lame or what?"

"They were wonderful!" breathed Phoebe.

Just then, a dude whom I would be forced by my extreme integrity to describe as handsome, approached us, smiling. He had these white teeth, and an expensive leather jacket and looked like he was Somebody. He had a press pass on his jacket. He flipped open his wallet to display ID.

"Hi, guys. Jason Haley, music critic for *Spin* magazine." He looked at Phoebe. "You were great tonight. Didn't catch your name."

"Me?" said Phoebe.

"Yes, you!"

"Phoebe."

"Just . . . Phoebe? Like Jewel or something?"

"Uh, no, Fortiere. Phoebe Fortiere," she whispered.

"Fabulous," said Jason Haley. "Hey, I'm out from New York, scouting new talent. Say, Phoebe, do you by any chance need a ride somewhere?"

"Actually, you do," said Ziggy. "There's no room in Veronica."

"Actually, then I guess I do," said Pheeb cautiously.

"Great!" said Jason Haley, taking Phoebe by the arm. "Come on, we got lots to talk about!" As they walked away, Phoebe looked back at me with a very solemn face.

And out front, the crowd continued to grow wilder and wilder, throwing chairs, screeching, laughing, cheering, and going generally mad. Right then and there was like the third worst moment of my entire life up until that point.

DogBreath was a loser. Not even a runner-up. Looked like I was gonna have to follow in my dad's footsteps.

Chapter Eighteen

The little purple Volkswagen sagged low to the ground—the backseat was crammed with amplifiers, drums, guitar cases, cables, and several months' worth of hamburger wrappers, milk shake cartons, and french fry boxes—and her suspension was not what it used to be. And, of course, in the passenger seat sat the giant Howie, the dog, in deep disgrace, his head stuck out the moon roof. Ziggy's skateboard was still tied to the car with a bungee cord. I was driving, totally illegally, because Zig's wrist still hurt.

"I'm so totally bummed, man," sighed Ziggy. "We was robbed. Really. Those guys that won, those Housewives—they're like just a novelty act. They only won because they're so weird."

"I know," I said.

"It's totally unfair," Zig went on. "We work and work and rehearse, and try to write really meaningful songs, and like our whole entire career depends on this contest, and along come some like tourist bunch of amateur chicks for God's sake and wreck the whole thing for us."

"This time," I said, "I think we should just wrap it up. Just quit for good."

"No, Timmer, no," said Ziggy. "It's not that bad. We're young. We're attractive. We'll have more chances."

"That's easy for you to say," I snapped. "You're not in love with Suzie Blethins. Your whole entire love life does not depend on our getting famous like mine does."

"Tim, did it ever occur to you that Suzie Blethins is not worthy to kiss the hem of your garment?" said Ziggy. "She is a total manipulative boozh. Dump her, man. She's not worth a moment of your precious time."

"Thanks for the advice, Dear Abby," I snarled.

After taking about a cautious hour to drive three miles to our house, I pulled up around the back so I wouldn't wake anybody up. The car sputtered, stalled, and died before I could even turn off the ignition. I got out of the car and went around to let Howie out.

"Looks like your mom's got company," Ziggy said.

"Huh," I said. "That's weird. She doesn't usually get any company this late."

"Maybe she's romantically involved with some tax consultant," said Ziggy.

I punched him on the arm. "Shut up, wouldja? Don't talk about my mom that way."

"Ow, you shouldn't hit an injured music god," said Ziggy.

"Then you shouldn't talk about my mom, okay? Now shut up and go home."

"How can I go home? I can't drive," he pointed out.

"Then what are your plans for the rest of the evening?"

"Me and Howie can stay at your place. Tomorrow morning you can take us home, okay?"

"My mom won't be too crazy about you and Howie staying over. You know how conservative she is," I reminded him.

"Well, just don't tell her, okay? We'll sneak in the back way. It'll be totally mystical. She won't even know we're there!"

"If it was just you it'd be mystical, maybe. Howie's so big, it's like trying to hide a beluga whale or something."

"Very droll, very amusant, I don't care about my feelings, but you shouldn't be mean to Howard. He's only a dumb beast," said Zig, hurt.

"That makes two of you. Come on, we have to sneak in the basement entrance real quiet. Make sure Howie stays quiet, too, or she'll kick you both out."

The three of us tried to quietly crunch across the gravel in the driveway so as not to make much noise. As it turned out, we didn't need to be so careful—there was 1970s rock music blasting in the living room. Rock music? In our living room? I was starting to feel apprehensive. What if some robbers had broken in and killed my mom and were looting our house while listening to the CD player?

We tiptoed to the basement door. I turned the key quietly in the lock, and the three of us tiptoed down the stairs, I guess, if a dog can tiptoe.

"Okay," I whispered, "I'm going to go up and check it out. You guys stay down here, okay?"

"Okay," said Ziggy. "Be careful, Timmer." He yawned deeply and headed off toward my room, Howie padding along behind him. Howie yawned, too.

"Come on in and lie down, Howie," Ziggy murmured.

I turned and snuck up the basement stairs that led to the kitchen. Just before I reached the kitchen door, I heard a woman scream. My God, I thought. Mom! I eased open the door. The kitchen was dark. I took a couple of cautious steps into the room.

There was another scream. My blood turned cold.

"Gimme some more champagne!"

"Jetta! Sit!"

I recognized Mrs. Lewis's voice.

Then Mrs. Lewis said, "Okay, everybody, and here's the big payoff!"

I snuck over to the living room archway but kept out of sight. My mom said, "Well, that's the car payment!"

Mrs. Lewis's voice said, "I'm donating my share to Bev. She's got a mortgage payment, too, you know."

"No, you're not!" my mom was heard to say.

"Yes, I am," said Mrs. Lewis. "And so is everybody else."

"That's right," said a chorus of women's voices. "This is for you, Bev!"

"I accept. You're all wonderful! And I'm going to pay you all back, every cent, I swear on Nick's grave! Wendy, you're brilliant! Everybody, I want to propose a toast!" I heard the dry pop of a champagne cork, then wine gurgling into glasses.

Curiosity got the better of me. I eased around the corner of the archway and into a dark corner of the living room. Bang, kapow. That was the sound of my mind imploding. Because, there, sitting around the living room, were the members of the Angry Housewives. Eeeeeek! Eeeeek! The bottom of the universe was whirling out into space from underneath me. Everything in my head was a black, swirling maelstrom of horror.

There was the woman with the baby-doll-head necklace, the lady with the toilet paper hair, the BBW lady with the keyboard, and the woman with the garbage sack dress. And they were, in order of appearance, Jetta, Wendy, Mrs. Lewis, and, of course, special guest star, my mom, Bev Threlfall—as 2000 Flushes.

I lurched. I staggered. My heart was pounding, and I felt a real, true, all-time mad flaring up out of my red-hot-poker-stabbed guts and the back of my brain into the front of my face. I felt like my eyes were twirling green headlights, and I felt like I had fangs popping out of my mouth, dripping scorching toxic saliva. I took several deep breaths.

In a burst of rage I burst to my feet and yelled out, "Traitor, traitor, traitor, traitor, traitor!"

My mom sat down on the couch very quickly and said, "—and then you marinate the beef for about fifteen minutes—"

"So *you're* the Angry Housewives," I howled. "God, I feel so stupid!"

"I can explain everything," said my mom.

"What is there to explain? I saw you there and so did everyone else," I shot back.

"She did it for you," said Mrs. Lewis.

"Oh, Timmy-Timmy," gurgled Jetta, lurching to her feet, "don't be mad at us. You're so cute!" Jetta staggered over in front of me. Her makeup was smeared, and she had a weird, half-insane smile on her face. She flung her arms around me, looked me deep in the eyes, then plunged her lips on mine and gave me a very intense, deep, and slurpy kiss. I felt cold horror flicker up and down my spine, much as I imagine how it feels to be electrocuted. It was horrible, like some Greek tragedy—Phaedra I think's the one I mean, thank you Mrs. Cederberg. Then Jetta fell back on the couch, her eyes closed.

I wiped my mouth with my sleeve. I was so angry I was almost on the verge of tears, but this time, all my pissed offness came hurling out.

"I can't believe you guys would be so low to even think about entering this contest! Mom, if you guys go on and do the finals, it'll ruin my life!"

"Oh, quit being so dramatic," said my mom.

"How can I show my face in school," I pleaded.

"Well, you don't show your face in school all that often as it is," Mrs. Lewis chimed in helpfully.

"Just don't admit I'm your mother," Mom said.

"You're not," I shouted. "A mother who loved me wouldn't do this!"

My mom got a strangely determined, defiant look on

her face. "I love you. But you know what? I love this band, too!"

I looked at my mom. Her bleached-blond wig, her garbage sack dress with Mr. Yuk stickers all over it, heavy black eye makeup, and scarlet red lipstick and nails.

"All this time, I was so worried about you, Mom," I said. "Thought you were still upset over Dad. But you were just planning to humiliate me."

I slammed out of the kitchen, ran down the stairs and into my room. Ziggy was asleep in my bed, snoring gently, curled up next to Howard. I flipped on the overhead light, grabbed a paper grocery sack, and started jamming clothes into it.

"Wake up, Zig! We're gettin' out of here!" I said. I grabbed a couple of books. Then I stopped.

Sitting on top of my bookcase was my teddy bear, Clarence, who I'd had since I was four. My dad had bought him for me at FAO Schwarz during a business trip to New York. Clarence was all raggedy and he was bald where I had chewed the fur off him, and he only had one eye, but I loved Clarence. I suddenly saw my dad's face, smiling at me.

It's funny, when someone you know really well dies or goes away, you think you'll always remember what they look like. Over the months, since Dad's death, his face was more and more vague in my mind. But now, I saw him smiling, pulling Clarence the bear out of his suitcase that first time. I remembered him picking me up, hugging me, kissing me.

My eyes stung with tears until Clarence got all swimmy. I picked him up and I stuck him on top of the paper bag.

Ziggy sat up sleepily, rubbing his eyes. "Where we goin'?"

"Your place."

"I like your place better."

"Tough. I'm not stayin' here one second longer. Get your clothes on. Wake Howie up and take him out to the car. I'll meet you out there in a few minutes."

"Couldn't we wait till tomorrow, man?"

"Now, Ziggy! Now!"

I ran outside and hot-wired Veronica's ignition and gunned the gas pedal. Nothing happened. I peered at the fuel gauge. Empty. Nothing was going right tonight.

I ran back inside and stomped into the living room. I stood there, defiant.

"I need some money. We're leaving," I said.

"Where are you going?" my mom asked, a quaver in her voice.

"To Ziggy's. I hope you sleep well tonight. His house has *rats!*"

"Tim, I'm not quitting this band. I'm sorry if things didn't go well for you tonight. But I have a life, too, you know. This is the most fun I've had since your father died. And if you don't like it, it's just too bad."

"Yeah, it is too bad," I said. "Well, you go right ahead on with your band, if that's what you want," I said. "Because you're never going to see me again. I'm leaving, and I'm leaving for good, and I never want to have anything to do with you. Or see you or talk to you or get a letter from you or anything. God, if Dad was alive, he would be so—so—I don't know what. Could you at *least* give us a ride to Ziggy's?"

"No," said Mom.

"Okay, we'll walk. But remember this: You're going to look really bad in my autobiography."

At that moment Ziggy came through the living room archway. Howie came padding along behind him. They were both still half asleep. Good old Ziggy. Sleeps in the nude. And he didn't have a stitch on. Talk about your nature boys.

"Hey, Tim, what're you doin' up here—urk! Why didn't you tell me somebody else was here?"

"Hey, I thought I told you to get up and get dressed! We're outta here!" I said.

All four of the women in the living room swiveled their heads toward Ziggy, did a double take at his pale nude form, screamed, and burst out laughing hysterically.

Ziggy was so sleepy, he barely registered what was going on for a second. Then he actually got a good look at all four women and stopped. He stared. His eyes got bigger and bigger. Then, finally, the penny dropped.

"Wow," he breathed. "You guys are the Angry Housewives! Far out!"

Chapter Nineteen

It was about three o'clock in the morning, the same night. We'd walked all the way to Ziggy's place, then fallen straight to sleep.

Suddenly, I was awake. A full moon shone through the window and into my face. Ziggy and Howard lay asleep on the futon next to me, both snoring.

I lay there on my side of the lumpy futon, thinking dark thoughts. My life had hit the complete bottom, the very worst it could ever get. I had known total and complete humiliation that night.

I thought maybe I could just go disappear somewhere—go shave my head bald and live in some Buddhist monastery on some remote Japanese island, living on rice and vegetables and running ten miles a day and meditating twelve hours a day and swimming in the ice-cold ocean and learning to play those giant taiko drums. Something like that. First I'd have to find enough money for a plane ticket to Japan. Nothing is ever easy.

Lying there in the dark, tormented by the demons of my recent past, I tried taking my mother's advice: I mentally surrounded my whole entire life with a pink balloon. I mentally let it float far away, out of sight, forever and ever. I mentally chanted, "My life is getting better and better." But it didn't work. Here I was, still trapped in my body, still in Ziggy's dark, dirty, rat-infested garage/apartment, still the laughingstock of the entire music scene of Seattle, and the despair of myself.

Try as I might, I couldn't think of a way out of this incredibly dark, tangled mess I was in the middle of. Suddenly, the image of Raquel Welch, dressed in her *One Million Years B.C.* fur bikini came bursting in my mind. She just stood there, squinting in the harsh, Paleolithic sunshine, woman enough for any challenge her primitive life might throw in her path. I pulled a legal pad out of my backpack and started writing a letter to Raquel:

Dear Ms. Welch:

Who am I? What am I? What is my purpose here on earth? My life is not getting better and better—it's getting worse and worse. My dad's dead, I'm broke, I'm in love with somebody who doesn't love me back, and my mom's band beat my band. What should I do?

Sincerely,
Timothy Threlfall

I slipped out of bed and put on my clothes. I started to tiptoe out of the door. Howard looked up at me through one half-opened eye.

"Go back to sleep, Howie," I whispered. Howie

heaved a sigh and flopped his head back down. I slipped out and closed the apartment door behind me.

Outside, the night was majestic. The sky was bright and clear, stars spangled across the horizon. A night breeze made rustling sounds in the maple trees along the street, and a night bird croaked. Up above me I could see the Big Dipper, and sighting along the forward edge of the cup, I found Polaris, the North Star, shining alone out in the center of the universe—it seemed to me like the still center point of a gyroscope, standing firm and strong as everything else spins around and around it. Everything changes but death and taxes and man's inhumanity to man and the North Star.

I walked down the Twelfth Street hill, under the shadow of the interstate, past the *Rocket* office, down toward the lake and the bridge. There was no traffic coming down Boyer; I crossed the street to the bridge against the red light.

I strolled out along the pedestrian lane on the west side of the span. The lake was quiet, lapping against the giant concrete piers that supported the bridge.

I walked out to the bridge mailbox, pulled it open, and looked inside. There it was, the photograph of Raquel in her fur bikini, defiant and alone against a world of mastodons, saber-tooths, and dinosaurs. I fished the letter out of my pocket and dropped it into the mailbox. I shut the mailbox, patted it, and said a little prayer: "Help me, Ms. Welch. You're my only hope."

I walked over to the bridge railing, leaned my elbows on the dusty green-painted metal, and looked down over the water. It was so peaceful and serene down there—nobody out there had a single care.

Down on the south bank of the lake, right in the shadow of the bridge, there was a little colony of houseboats. Most of them were dark at this time of night, but one still had a few lights on. A man stood out on the houseboat deck, playing a clarinet. The soft, nasal, mellow sound spiraled up into the starry night, and suddenly I felt peace in my heart. I had a feeling, a sure thing feeling, that somehow everything would get better.

Fwappeta, fwappeta, fwappeta, a police helicopter swooped down over the lake, aiming a spotlight at something out on the dark water, and *fwappeta, fwappeta,* they were gone. The lake was quiet once again.

The soft putta-putta of an expensive outboard motor announced the arrival of a tall sailboat coming around the corner of the lake shore, probably heading for a moorage somewhere in Lake Washington. Her sails were furled and she was running under power. A lone man stood on the deck of the big sailboat, steering her from the afterdeck wheel. Her mainmast was over fifty feet tall—they'd have to open the bridge to let her pass.

The man with the clarinet waved at the man on the sailboat. The man on the sailboat waved back. As the sailboat neared the bridge, the skipper shifted the boat engine to neutral, and gave two short, sharp honks on his boat horn, signaling the night-shift bridge operator that he wanted to pass underneath the bridge.

From up in the dimly lit bridge tower, the operator honked back, signaling the boat skipper that he'd be opening the bridge in a few seconds. Whoever the operator was, I know it wasn't that traitor Wendy, because for all I knew she was still livin' it up over at my house.

I looked down onto the boat deck. The man below looked about as big as a jelly bean.

Abruptly, a few yards away from me, the bridge's warning bell started dinging. The yellow guard arms began slowly, mechanically, to unfold and reach across toward each other, to prevent the traffic from driving onto the bridge. Except at three in the morning, there wasn't any traffic.

I started to turn and leave the bridge. And then, I turned back. Here was my chance to live out one of my lifelong fantasies—here was my chance to ride the bridge all the way up into the starry night sky. Why not? There was no traffic. It was dark on the bridge deck—the bridge tender would never see me, and the boat below wouldn't, either. I could hear Raquel telling me that I needed to do something extraordinary, something risky and dangerous, something momentous, to turn the tide of my life. Riding the bridge up into the night seemed to be a likely deed, a beau geste, a key to turn the dead bolt in the triple-locked door that stood between me and my good fortune.

Heart pounding, I slipped my fingers through the crisscross, steel mesh that stretched between the metal posts along the sides of the bridge.

There are times when time seems to stand still. At first, this was one of those times.

But I could remember, like in a dream, the main points. Slowly, slowly, the bridge deck split across the middle.

Slowly, slowly, the bridge raised up, an inch at a time, the warning bell playing a ding-ding accompaniment. In a few more seconds I couldn't stand upright anymore, as the bridge deck tilted past a forty-five degree slant and kept moving. I hooked my toes into the metal mesh below my feet. I heard wind in the trees. I heard traffic on the interstate overpass. I heard the warning bell dinging.

In a few more heartbeats, the bridge deck was fully upright, and I was hanging high, high up in the air, dangling from the guardrail. I slipped my toes out of the mesh so I could dangle free in the air for a few seconds. The wind whistled past my ears. The full moon reflected down on the ruffly lake. It was awesome. Below me, the giant sailboat glided majestically underneath the bridge. The fog light on the mainmast passed just a few yards in front of my nose. The metal dug into my clenched fingers—my hands started to feel numb in the cold night air. But I clung hard, riding the giant up into the stars—nothing is won by those who give up too easy, by those who just let go.

Suddenly, the whole mood was spoiled by a bossy, bratty voice coming over the bridge PA system—

"Please—hang on! Help is on the way! Don't jump! Don't let go! Think of all you have to live for! If nothing else, try to remember that committing suicide is illegal. I've called for help!"

Suicide? Me? Boy, did they have me figured wrong!

The bridge stayed where it was, open wide and high up in the air. Why didn't the stupid bridge tender lower the thing? How much longer did they think I could stay up here like this? I heard horns honking. Down below, backed up behind the guardrails, a handful of cars waited to cross the bridge. Somebody shouted, "Hey, kid! Look over this way and wave!"

I looked—somebody flashed a camera. Somebody else had a video camcorder trained on me. Great. Just great.

Then, once again, I heard, far away but getting closer, the *fwappeta, fwappeta* of another helicopter. Then it got very, very loud. The black-and-white police 'copter rounded the bridge tower and came into view just above me. The downdraft practically knocked me off my perch. I looked up, and suddenly I was looking into the glare of a million-watt spotlight. I saw a rope ladder being slowly lowered down from the open hatch of the helicopter. And I heard a voice over a bullhorn: "This is the Seattle Police Department. Please move slowly and carefully. Put one hand at a time on the rope ladder, hang on tight, place your feet below you, then we will assist you into the aircraft."

Well, as I saw it, my options were (a) to stay where I was, (b) climb up the ladder, or (c) jump off the bridge into the lake about thirty feet below.

If I stayed there, or climbed up the ladder, I was bound to go to jail—or something. Option *c* didn't look very good, either. Who knew how deep the water was there? Well, it was deep enough for the big ships to go through. So, great deeds and all, you know.

Don't try this at home, kids. I swung around to the other side of the bridge railing, took a deep breath, said another, a who knew, maybe final, prayer, and let go. And hurtled like a stone toward the lake.

Chapter Twenty

"Timmer, star-baby, music-man—open up the sleepy peepers, man! Take a look at what's on Mr. Television!"

The voice came from far, far away, through layers of fog and fatigue. Slowly I rose to the surface. I tried to open my eyes, but they felt glued shut. I felt hands shaking me roughly. I felt a raspy tongue slobbering across my cheeks, and hot doggy breath in my face. I forced my eyes open a tiny slit. For a minute I couldn't remember where I was.

Slowly awareness seeped in—I was at Ziggy's place, sleeping on the lumpiest futon in lumpy futon history. Howie was straddling me, blissfully licking my loathly face. Ziggy stood next to him, shaking my arm. I heard the mumble, mumble of the little TV set. Ziggy shoved a glass of Tang into my hand. Howie bumped it and nearly slopped it all over me, the blanket, and the lumpy futon. Ziggy punched my shoulder and said, "Dude, you gotta see this!"

I rolled over and coughed. The lake hadn't agreed

with my upper respiratory system. I opened my eyes a milli-slit wider, and focused weakly on the TV, with its little clump of aluminum foil bunched around the top of the rabbit ears. There was some footage of a rock band on the screen, and a commentator's voice: ". . . the surprise hit of the evening. Farland Chang was there with our camera crew, and has this report. Farland?"

A blow-dried Asioid-American dude, so out he was in, came slithering onto the screen.

"Kathy, Saturday night, the Dirt Club, Seattle's premiere rock music venue, was the wild scene of a surprise upset in a hotly contested local Battle of the Bands! Appearing out of nowhere to sweep the competition was the astonishing new group, the Angry Housewives, a sensational all-girl band who ripped up the place with their hilarious, bad-to-the-bone rendition of a song, which we can only refer to on screen as 'Eat Your Blankety-Blank Cornflakes.'

"And, like a combination of Julius Caesar and Cinderella, they came, they sang, they conquered, and they disappeared before anybody could find out who they really are. So, 2000 Flushes, Numzit, Charmin, and Brillo—wherever you are, whoever you are, you won the contest, and we all expect you back next week for the finals. Lewd Fingers, owner of the Dirt Club, says his office, and the *Rocket,* are being besieged by phone calls and requests to find out more about this hot new group! And the *Rocket* is planning to run a special two-page interview and article. Back to you, Kathy."

The blond coanchorperson shook her head wryly, laughing with her coanchor. "Heh, heh, heh—eat your cornflakes! What'll they think of next, Farland? In other news, police are still searching for a young man who tied up late night traffic when he dangled off the University Bridge two nights ago, and then plunged into the lake. According to an apparent suicide note discovered in the bridge mailbox, addressed to Raquel Welch, the person may go by the name of—hmm, hard to read his handwriting—Jiminy Jrelfall."

Here, they started running the videotape of me clinging onto the bridge deck high in the air. Fortunately, the searchlight had been so bright on my face, and I had been so far away from the *Live from Five* videocam, you couldn't really tell it was me too much.

The anchor continued: "Attempts to drag the lake bottom have not turned up a body yet, but the search will continue. If you recognize this person, please call the Seattle police. They say no crime was committed, but jumping from a Seattle bridge is punishable by a fine and imprisonment if the presiding judge determines that life or limb was endangered by the person's act—"

"Oh, my goddess," said Ziggy. He grabbed my Tang and finished it in one gulp.

"Do you have anything to eat around here?" I croaked.

"Doritos. Peanut butter. You want some peanut butter? It's a little bit old."

"Skip it," I said. "Don't you have any bacon and eggs or something?"

"You know I'm a vegetarian, man," said Zig huffily.

Another anchor, Harry Wappler, came on the screen, looking like he was getting ready to announce the end of the world: "We interrupt the noon news for a live King 5 exclusive news bulletin. King 5's reporters have discovered that 2000 Flushes, the leader of the smash hit band, the Angry Housewives, is actually a mature Seattle woman named Beverly Threlfall, AKA 2000 Flushes. We take you live to the scene outside Ms. Threlfall's attractive Montlake residence."

"What time is it, man?" I croaked.

"It's 10 A.M. Monday morning, dude—you've been asleep for like a day and a half!"

As I lay there, trying to take everything in, suddenly, there on the TV screen was the outside of our house. There was a smallish mob of teenagers outside, milling around, calling for my mom to come out.

Then the Montego drove up, and Mom got out, carrying a bag of groceries, mostly boxes of macaroni and cheese. When she saw the rabble, she tried to get back into the car, but the reporter ran over and shoved the microphone in her face.

"Hello, Ms. Threlfall! May I call you 2000 Flushes?"

"What?" my mother croaked. "Oh, my gosh—those bikers that followed us home last night—they must have told where we live!"

"How does it feel to be a famous rock star?"

"What?" my mother repeated, even more dazed.

"Looks like you've got a little fan club already!" said Farland Chang.

"Ulp!" said my mother. "My life is getting better and better—"

"Excuse me?" said the reporter.

Suddenly Mom jumped back in the Montego, slammed the door, gunned the motor, and peeled out of the driveway before the crowd could stop her.

The reporter looked at the camera. "Sudden fame is . . . not always easy to handle. Join us live at seven tonight when psychologist Marjorie Mamet discusses strategies for stressless success. This is Farland Chang, live for TV Five. Back to you, Kathy."

Just then, the street door to Zig's apartment was heard by us to slam open. Several hundred pairs of loud clumpy shoes were heard by us to thunder up the stairs. Ziggy's face went white, even whiter than usual.

"It's the fans, Timmy. They've found us. They're going to murder us! Quick, block the door. Kill, Howard! Kill!"

Ziggy went and tried to block the door. Howard sat there panting, smiling, his tongue hanging out. The door banged open anyway, scattering Ziggy like a leaf in an autumnal blast. Todi and Flipper stormed into the bleak apartment, like twin Zeus the Thunderers. They had both shaved their heads bald.

"You're bald, men!" hiccuped Ziggy. "You're wearing all black!"

"We're in mourning for our life!" shouted Todi.

Flipper held up a copy of the *Rocket* and shook it in our faces.

"Look, man! Look! The *Rocket* just came out. Special edition. Look who's plastered all over the front cover!"

We duly looked. And it was my incognito mom, plus her three friends dressed in their grunge gear, who were plastered all over the cover. The picture was a candid news shot of the Angry Housewives at the Dirt Club, with Jetta screaming and throwing cornflakes. The headline read: FRENETIC FLOOZY CHANTEUSIE FEMMES FAN FLAMES OF FIERCELY FLAILING FANOMANIACS. DETAILS INSIDE."

"These guys work fast," said Ziggy.

We flipped open the paper and read: "Far and away the most exciting band to emerge from Saturday's contest was the Angry Housewives!! The all-gal group, with a kamikaze cutting-edge style, stunned the crowd at the Dirt Club. Lead singer Numzit screamed like a banshee, lurching about the stage, hurling abuse and cornflakes at the thunderstruck crowd.

"Also of interest was debut group DogBreath, featuring a real live dog, a very interesting Phoebe Fortiere doing vocal chores on 'Hell School,' and the first-ever mosh pit dive by a drummer where nobody in the underwhelmed crowd bothered to catch the diver."

"I hate the press," said Ziggy.

"Nice, huh?" said Todi. "Real nice."

"Me, I'm moving to Tacoma," said Flipper. "I can't even go onstage around here anymore. I'd get laughed out of town."

"You guys," Ziggy said. "You're both kick-ass musicians. You guys are the breath of DogBreath. We can't go on without you."

"What's to go on? DogBreath stinks," said Todi. "We're leavin'."

"Yeah," said Flipper. "Look at ol' Tim here. He's totally demoralized and debased and humiliated and raped and pillaged. None of us will ever play again. We're through."

They turned to leave. Just then, Ziggy's dad hollered from the main house.

"Don Ameche* comin' across, Siegmund!"

Ziggy can't afford a phone, and his dad won't pay to have one put in Ziggy's garage/apartment. But last year, his dad rigged up a clothesline and a pulley and a basket, so that he could send the cellular phone out to the garage if there's a call for Ziggy. There was a call for Ziggy.

"Hello?" said Ziggy into the phone. "Oh, hi, Mrs. Judas. Here, Tim, it's your mom."

"I'm not speaking to her ever again," I said bleakly.

"He's not speaking to you, Mrs. Judas. Okay, I'll— what? From who? Are you putting me on? What's the phone number? Thanks!"

Ziggy turned to us, a slightly glazed look in his eye.

"DogBreath is in the finals! We're in the finals, man! Supposed to call Lewd Fingers."

Ziggy punched in the number three times before he got through, he was so nervous.

"Hello, Mr. Fingers? This is Siegmund Jones, drummer of DogBreath. You called?"

Ziggy sat and listened for a moment. "All right! Fabuloso! Oh, yeah, I see. Okay. Next Saturday night at eight. And don't be late. See you!"

"We're in, fellows!" crowed Zig. "We made the contest! And this time—this time, we're gonna win!"

---

*A late movie actor named Don Ameche once played the role of Alexander Graham Bell in a biopic. Hence, older Americans used to refer to the telephone as a "Don Ameche."

"How in the name of Jimi did we make it? We did horrible!" said Todi.

"By default, boys, by default. The three runner-ups all got disqualified. Beata Tomboy Sundown accidentally crushed her lead guitarist in the mosh pit. Payperkutz had all their equipment stolen. Swollen Monkeez had all their equipment repossessed. We're next on the lineup."

"If we really practice hard this week," Flipper said, "maybe we *can* win."

"Against this? Are you brain damaged?" asked Todi, waving the *Rocket* in front of me.

"Look at this band, the Angry Housewives! They like, drove everybody around the bend. It was like the second coming of, I don't know, like, well, I don't know. They can do no wrong. We don't have a chance!"

"Oh, and guess what, lads," said Ziggy. "Guess whose mother is the rhythm guitarist for the Angry Housewives?"

"Who??" chorused Todi and Flipper.

"Ms. Beverly Judas Threlfall, Senior—mother to our little friend Timmer here."

"What??" chorused Todi and Flipper, spinning to look at me with gimlet eyes, whatever those are. "What?? That band is your MOTHER??" Slowly they turned, step-by-step—"Why we oughtta kill you with our bare—we oughtta rip out your—grrrrr!"

"Grrrrrrrrr!" said Howie, taking a step toward the boys. The boys took a step back.

"Watch your tone of voice around Howie, guys. See? Look, there on the TV," said Ziggy helpfully. "They're replaying the newscast. See Tim's house. See Tim's mom.

See Tim's mom drive away from the house very, very fast. Drive, Mom, drive!"

"So *that's* why she'd never let us practice in your basement! She was worried about the competition!" yelled Flipper.

"I don't think so," I said. "They'll probably drop out before the second contest! They're always dropping out of stuff."

"Timmer's right, guys. His mom's a flake."

"She always speaks highly of you, Siegmund," I said.

"I mean that as a compliment," Ziggy lied. "But! We gotta concentrate on trying to win this next contest. They really liked Phoebe. I think she's the key here."

Todi turned to look at me again. Suddenly I saw how he might look in twenty years. Fat, mean, bald, mowing his lawn.

"First things first, man. If we go on with the band, that chick goes. She's out."

"Ditto for me," said Flipper.

"I fail to see the problem," Ziggy said. "The press loves her—they picked right up on her."

"Boy, did they ever," I said. "She took off with that critic from *Spin*." Something inside my chest area did a kind of weird jealousy squeeze as I spoke.

"Yeah, see? And she's creative. She's weirdly unique. She sings good. The crowd really responds to her."

"Fine, let them respond to her in some other band," said Flipper. "I do not wanna be associated as no chick band. I wanna play songs about cars and beer and freaking out and weird sex and beating people up and scarification and diesel fuel and tattoos and stuff. She wants to play songs about love and her damn emotions."

"Yeah," said Todi. "Love and emotions. What kind of crap is that? Is this not the twenty-first century? Are we not men?"

"We are Devo," said Ziggy irrelevantly.

"You are a ponce, man," said Todi. "Come on, Flipper, let's blow this fruit stand."

"Are we gonna practice this week?" I asked.

"Call us when your mom's band drops out. Then we'll talk," said Flipper. "The Angry Housewives. Fudge." He turned to go. "'Mon, Todi."

"Loser!" Todi hollered back at me over his shoulder.

They clomped down the stairs and disappeared into the gray morning.

Chapter Twenty-one

The TV started playing *Live with Regis and Kathie Lee.* When Kathie Lee came on screen, Howie started barking at her.

"Quiet, Howsie," said Ziggy.

"Zig," I asked, "what do you think about Phoebe?"

"Phoebe's sheer genius, man. You know I dig her entirely. She's a tower of gold. But, if the guys don't want her in the band, well, I don't know."

"All of a sudden you're taking their side?"

"Not really, man. But look, DogBreath is not like this Thing, see. DogBreath is like more like an Idea. A Concept. It's greater than any one individual member. Keeping the band together is more important than Phoebe or you or me."

"So you think we should dump our resident genius to keep those two Neanderthals in the band?"

"Does Phoebe play an instrument, Monsieur Einstein?"

"A little guitar, maybe," I said.

"Todi and Flipper leave, we got two singers, lead guitar and drums. Phoebe leaves, we got a singer, bass, rhythm guitar and lead guitar, plus amps and equipment. You see the problem."

"I get it," I said. "But I don't see why we can't just keep everybody. At least for one more week."

"That's democracy in action for ya, Timmy."

Regis Philbin laughed heartily at something their guest Marilu Henner had said. Howie growled at him.

"I gotta take Howie for a walk," said Ziggy. "Be back in a flash."

I dragged over to the sink and splashed cold water on my face.

I tried thinking for a few minutes. What to do next. What to do with my life. Where to live. How I would get from where I was to fame, fortune, a life of luxury and prestige. I mean even the remaining members of ratty bands like the Sex Pistols live in fabulous villas in the south of France. Is that so much to ask in life?

Everybody in my band was totally alienated.

I felt terrible. Like I was on some nightmare national television program on an emergency broadcast, in the brightest spotlight in the world, with a big sign pinned on my chest saying LOSER with a million arrows pointing at me, and everybody on the planet watching. Loser, loser, loser.

Thinking didn't do any good. Doctor Powerhead always says thinking *never* does any good. He always cites an obscure Chinese philosophical work called the *Tao Te Ching,* which he says means "The Book of the Virtuous Path." He always says, "Don't think. Thinking gets you in trouble. Just be." Another quote is "Those of superlative virtue are all very simple people. Eliminate your pride and desires and get rid of your airs and ambitions, for they will be of no benefit to you."

Fine, but I'm not old enough to have superlative virtue. First I want my Alfa Romeo Spider XKT-200 in midnight blue with thirty milliliter tires and an overhead camshaft. And fame and fortune in a rock band. And Suzie Blethins. *Then* I'll shave my head and go live in a Zen monastery.

As I was nonthinking these thoughts, I heard steps coming up. I figured it was Ziggy. I splashed more cold water on my face and my pits. I looked for desodorissant, but Zig doesn't believe in it. Or can't afford it. I was looking for toothpaste and finding only anchovy paste, when I heard a familiar plugged-up-nose voice—

"Hi, Tib. Cad I cub id?"

I turned to see Phoebe in the doorway. She was carrying a guitar case.

"Sure, come on—"

Then I realized I was still in my underwear. I grabbed my jeans, which were still slightly damp, and covered with dog hair and lake weeds. I slipped them on.

"—in."

Phoebe came in, kind of slow and a little thoughtful. She was wearing a long black raincoat that dragged on the ground as she walked.

"Can I talk to you?" she asked.

"Yeah, sure."

"Can I ask you something?"

"I said, yeah."

"Are you okay?" she inquired.

"Am I okay? Let me think that one over a minute. No, I am not okay. My life is ruined."

"I think you're too young and talented and nice for your life to be really ruined. Everything will work out."

"Thank you for the thought. However, there's something you may not know yet about Saturday night's debacle."

"What?"

"My mother and her three best friends are the Angry Housewives. DogBreath was beaten and humiliated by my mother and her middle-class, suburbanoid friends."

"I know."

"You—how did you know?"

"I called over there this morning. There was no answer, so I took a bus over to see you. There was a crowd of people over there—fans. I managed to get in the house. Your mother is desperate. She's really sorry. She needs you."

"She should have thought of that before she betrayed us."

"She knows that now. Tim, why don't you go home? Your mom doesn't know anything about the music business. I think she just really really needs you."

"Oh, let her call Lewd Fingers or Chainsaw Records or somebody. They can tell her all about the music business." I glared at Phoebe.

She wasn't wearing her glasses and she'd done something different with her hair—just slicked it back or something. You could see her face better. She had nice skin. Kind of translucent. No zits. And I'd never really noticed her lips before. Kind of like chiseled like a Greek statue lady. Like kind of classic. She peered at me hopefully one last time.

"Okay. But if you change your mind—"

"I'm not gonna change my mind."

"Okay. Um, okay. Well, I better go."

"Okay, Phoebe."

"Uh, but . . . actually, Tim, I was going to ask you— would you, would you mind listening to this song I'm working on? There's something wrong with it, but I can't figure out what. Maybe you could give me some suggestions."

"Maybe you'd better ask somebody else. I obviously don't know anything about writing songs."

"Tim, just tell me your honest opinion, okay?"

She started to strum the guitar in the girl-folk-rock thing they do. She sang, in her weird breathy little voice:

"Girls don't care about your hair
'Bout what you wear, about your car
Girls just care 'bout who you are—
Inside

"Boys don't care how bad you feel
If love is real, or if it's not
Boys don't care 'cause boys have got
Their pride

"Girls don't know why boys are bad
Girls just know it makes them sad
Boys may look but
They don't see
That's why boys can be so lonely

"Boys don't care till it's too late
To change their ways and change their fate
Won't give their hearts—no they don't
have a prayer—
But boys don't boys don't boys don't boys
don't care!"

When Phoebe got done singing, she sat there, still for a minute, thinking, doodling on the guitar strings. I didn't say anything at all—I didn't trust myself to, because my throat felt kind of funny and choky. Then she looked up at me. Her blue eyes looked kind of swimmy and out of focus, as usual. I never noticed how long her eyelashes were before.

"Well? What's wrong with it?" she asked.

"Wrong with it? Nothing. It's great. It's a great song. The music is great. The chords are great. The hook is great. The structure is interesting. It's great."

"It's not as good as your songs," she said.

"It's better. It's a lot better than my songs. I mean, I don't know what you mean, what do you *think* is wrong with it?"

"I don't know. It makes me feel sad when I sing it."

"That's *good*. That's what we want. Emotions."

"No, it isn't."

"Yes, it is. Look, I think if it started out folky-guitary like that, then went into this real hard rock thing—the music would really be screaming along—'boys don't boys don't boys don't caaaaaaarrrrrrrrrre!!!' Wow. It like rips your guts out with angst and despair. I think Dog-Breath should do this song."

"But I didn't write it for DogBreath, I wrote it—I wrote it for y—"

"Phoebe, it's a brilliant song. We're going back again Saturday night, and with this song—"

"Todi and Flipper don't want me back. They want me out."

"Did they say that to you?"

"No. But I can tell."

"I'm the leader of the band. I make those decisions. I want the song in. It's in. You're in. Ah—ah—ah—choo!"

Suddenly I was caught in a fit of sneezing. I felt hot. I started shivering.

"Tim, you're catching a cold!" Phoebe said. She put the back of her hand on my forehead. Suddenly, my teeth started to chatter. My dunk in the lake was catching up to me.

"You better get back under the covers, Tim. I'll make you some tea or something."

"Z-Z-Z-Ziggy doesn't have any tea. All he has is Tang and peanut butter and tortilla chips."

"Well, I'll make you some hot Tang then. Here, get back under." Phoebe tucked me in, her blue swimmy eyes concerned. She went over to the hot plate and boiled some water, added some Tang, and brought it over to the futon.

"Here, drink this. It's got lots of Vitamin C."

I took a swallow, then was overtaken by another fit of shivers. Phoebe took the cup out of my hand and set it on the floor.

"You need to get warm, Tim. Here, here's some White Flower Oil." She fished in her bag and pulled out a little glass jar with Chinese letters and a blue screw top. She undid the bottle, tapped it against her fingers. Then she rubbed the stuff under my nostrils. Sheets of flame seemed to rush up my nose.

"Yow, what *is* that stuff? It's really intense!"

"Chinese medicine. It'll heat your meridians up. Meanwhile I better call your mother. You probably need to go to the doctor."

"No, not my mother. I'm not speaking to my mother."

Even through the fever and the White Flower Oil, I could smell that faint little smell of roses Phoebe always had. It smelled like the garden of Allah, the Arabian Nights. Her body lay warm against mine outside the blanket. With her hair slicked back, her stupid blue glasses gone, she didn't look so juvenile. She didn't look like the little sister I never had. She looked—beautiful. How could I have been so completely stupid? Here was the woman of my dreams all along. How could I have ever even cared about Suzie Blethins?

"Phoebe," I started. I turned my face toward hers. Gently I reached to kiss her. "Phoebe," I repeated.

And then I passed out.

Chapter Twenty-two

Seattle rain. Buckets and buckets of gray, slanting wet, splashing down, puddling up, and running along the sidewalks and gushing into the gutters. It was the Saturnight of the final contest, and I was pulling our gear out of Veronica. The rain made life very poetic, and very pathetic, and very wet.

I and Ziggy had gotten Todi and Flipper to agree to play one last time together. They weren't happy about it, they weren't nice about it, but they agreed. They even agreed to Phoebe, if it was one last time. And that was fine with me. If DogBreath won this contest, we could get ourselves a new couple of sidemen anywhere—*nice* ones.

The sound system at the Dirt Club was throbbing away at about thirty-nine on your volume dial. I clunked down the amplifier I was trying to drag in through the loading bay. Ziggy appeared in the alley doorway.

I hauled the cables and mike stands backstage and began plugging in plugs.

"Yo."

"Hey."

I looked up. Todi and Flipper stood there, very surly, very defensive, but they had their gear with them, and showed every sign of cooperating with us artistically. Fine. We would use them as long as they were useful to us. I hunkered down, splicing together two frayed cords with some duct tape. Suddenly Ziggy came running up, and nearly knocked me over.

"Emergency, Tim. You gotta drive me over to the school like ASAP!"

"Man, what is it?" I said. "There's no time."

"My dress, man. My lucky dress! I left my lucky dress in Natasha's locker at school! Come on, man, let's go! We can get there in five minutes!"

"His dress," said Todi.

"Fruit loops, totally," said Flipper.

"What do you need that freaking dress for?" I asked. "You look just fine the way you are. Thermal underwear becomes you."

"Man, Natasha gave me that dress. I was wearing that dress when we started this band. It's like my talisman! My lucky charm. I can't play for dog doo without my lucky dress. Drive me, drive me, drive me!"

"I've never known you to be superstitious, Zig. If you truly need that dress, then drive yourself," I said. "If we're not set up by contest time, we're dead meat."

"My wrist still hurts. If I drive I can't drum. If I drum I can't drive."

Todi glared at me. "Would you for crud's sake drive him? Otherwise we'll never get onstage."

"Oh, man, oh man, oh goddess," I hollered. "My life is getting—better and better. My life is getting better and better . . . Come on, my Ziggy. Let's go. But we're gonna drive fast, okay? So fasten your figurative seat belt."

Ziggy grabbed his skateboard, we hurled ourselves into Veronica, and Ziggy, me, and Howie Indy 500'ed over to the school.

As we screamed into the visitors' parking lot, Ziggy noted a very curious thing—there were about a zillion cars parked there, and two or three buses. Why were so many people here during the evening? Community art class? Senior citizen tai chi or yogaerobics? PTA? Children of Single Parents Sock Hop and Silent Auction? Who knew?

"Look, Zig!" I said. "Over there! Jean, the sado/maso/psycho-killer forty-five-year-old bus driver."

I pointed to where Jean stood lounging against her school bus, smoking a Virginia Slims menthol cigarette and picking her teeth with a jackknife. The bus idled gently behind her, diesel exhaust puffing up into the soggy air.

"We're gonna have to go in the back way," said Zig. "There's too many people here. I just know something will go wrong if anybody sees us."

"Why?" I asked. "We're not going to do anything wrong. We're just gonna get your damn dress outta the damn locker, then scram."

"If something doesn't go wrong," said Zig.

"What could go wrong?" I asked naively.

"Murphy's Law," he said, lighting a cigarette and coughing. *"'If something can go wrong, it will. And at the worst possible time.'"*

"Don't be such a pessimist," I said. "Come on, let's go!"

"Gimme my skateboard." I did so.

We hurried around the back entrance to the school. A big sign said, WELCOME, DIXY LEE RAY HIGH ALUMS. RECEPTION AND DANCE IN THE ALL-PURPOSE ROOM.

We pulled open the door and started inside.

"Tickets?" I and Ziggy whirled around to be confronted by Marjorie Mamet, the ticket taker for the dance.

"Well, hi there, Milo! And who's your little friend?"

"Milo?" croaked Zig.

"Siegfried," I said.

"Oh, right!" said Ms. Mamet. "You and I have an appointment, I think, Siegfried! I'm really looking forward to that! But what in the world are you doing in the building after hours?" she asked.

"Study hall," I said. "We have a special extracurricular study hall tonight for the SAT exams. Gotta run."

As we ran down the hall, we heard a scream and a familiar bark.

"Oh, my God—Howie's following us," said Ziggy. "Hurry."

"Somebody get that dog outta here," we heard a male voice calling from somewhere behind us.

We raced around the corner to the staircase, and went pounding up to the second floor. Our lockers were close to the administrative office and the trophy case and the men's faculty bathroom. Ziggy loped down the hall to Natasha's locker. He twirled the dial. He yanked the handle. Nothing happened.

"Hurry up, Zig!" I urged.

"I can't remember the combination!" he said. He twirled the dial some more—"Twenty-seven right, five left, fifteen right—bingo!" Ziggy yanked the door open. The locker, except for a bunch of old food, gym socks and jockstrap, and piles of wet comic books, was empty.

"Woof!" Howie came prancing up to us, ecstatic at seeing us again after such a protracted absence.

"Where's my lucky dress? Where's my dress?" Ziggy asked.

"I don't know. It's not here. Can we please go now?"

"I know where it is," Ziggy said. He looked at me, his eyes narrowing. "It's in Thompson's office."

"I'm not going in there," I said.

"I am," Ziggy said. He ran down two doors to the Boys' Club counselor's office, Howie leaping along behind him, trailing saliva. Ziggy grabbed the door handle and pulled. Nothing happened.

"It's locked," Ziggy yelped. He peered through the frosted glass, trying futilely to see inside.

"Of course it's locked, you dolt," I said.

A haunted, wild look took fire in Ziggy's eyes.

"My dress! Stolen by the bourgeois pigs! I must have it! Storm the Bastille! Power to the people, right on!"

Ziggy lifted his skateboard high over his head and brought it crashing down through the door window. Glass splintered and flew through the air, smashed to the floor, and went skimming and skittering and tinkling along the polished linoleum hallway.

"Jesus gosh, Zig! Are you crazy? Are you hopelessly insane?"

"No longer!" he cried. He dashed into the office and emerged a few seconds later, his dress clutched triumphantly in his hand. "Hello, dress! Thank you, goddress, for my dress! Come on, Ymmit! Back to the club! Now, with dress in hand, DogBreath shall be victorious!"

We started back for the stairs. A tenor voice brought us to a standstill.

"And just what do you gentlemen think you're doing?"

The familiar face and form came toward us, wearing a cheap wrinkled suit I'm guessing from Men's Wearhouse.

"Cheezit! It's Mr. Thompson," I yelled. "Head for the front stairs!"

"Woof!" said Howie.

"Gentlemen, I'd advise you to stop right there! Breaking and entering, damaging private property, bringing unauthorized large animals onto the premises—"

Ziggy flung his skateboard onto the polished linoleum. With a single mind, we jumped on the board and started swoofing down the hall at top speed, Howie galloping along beside.

"Stairs, man!" We came around the corner, deboarded, and went sliding down the bannister, executing the double-front nollie rail backslide down to the first landing.

"Gentlemen, come back! I'm warning you!" Thompson's voice came echoing down the stairs. As we came to the bottom landing, we heard the sounds of music wafting from the Cafetorium. A glimpse through the half-open door across the hall revealed balloons, star-spangled crepe paper, and middle-aged couples slow dancing. A recording of the Carpenters drifted out into the hall-way—"*Sha la la la, whoa-oh-oh*"— et cetera, et cetera.

"Stop those kids and that dog!" Thompson was at the top of the stairs. Coming down the hall toward us was Marjorie Mamet.

"Is something wrong? What's going on?" she asked.

"Oh, we're just doing our role-playing game with Mr. Thompson. It's called 'Thinking on Your Feet.' It's part of the SAT test."

"I may look stupid," said Ms. Mamet. "But I've got news for you. I'm not. I have a Ph.D. in social work. And I know a problem when I see one. A boy. A dress. Sexual identity crisis. Right?"

"What?" Ziggy said.

"It's very common for young men in our society to have gender anxiety. To heck with the dance. Let's talk about this, right here, right now. There's nothing to be ashamed of. It happens to more people than you would imagine. My office is right this way. But first let's have a big hug."

"Maybe next week," I hollered. I grabbed Ziggy. "Come on, Zig. Or we're busted. Let's get outta here!"

"Woof!" said Howie.

At that moment Mr. Thompson came huffing and puffing down the stairs. "Stop those boys!" he hollered.

Mr. Fredericks, the history teacher and football coach, came out of the Cafetorium.

"What's the problem, Jim?" he asked Thompson.

"Those boys—vandalized my office!" he said. "Grab them!"

"All right, troops! Front and center! What have you got to say for yourselves?" Mr. Fredericks said to our retreating backsides.

Bang, kapow, I and Ziggy and Howie ran through the front door, down the steps, and around the corner to the parking lot. We did a one-hundred-yard dash to Veronica and leaped inside. Ziggy put the two wires together. Nothing happened. He jiggled the wires some more. He got a mild shock—yipes!—but nothing happened, engine-wise. No turning over. No starting.

"God! We're out of gas! Or something." We looked at each other. We looked at Howie. Howie smiled and drooled.

"Stop those boys!" voices came from the building. We looked up to see Jean, the bus driver, who must have driven alums to the dance, go dogtrotting over toward the school building, apparently to check out the ruckus.

Ziggy looked at me intensely.

"Timmer, this is our big night. That is our big bus. Let's get going immédiatemente."

"We can't, Ziggy."

"Yes, we can. They do it in the movies all the time. Come on, Flash, let's went."

We flung out of the veedub and ran for the bus, Ziggy panting like a man on the moon without a space helmet. Up the steps into the bus, one, two, three, four, five. Howie, too.

"You drive, man," said Zig. "My wrist still hurts."

I slid into the driver's seat. The engine was still idling. I grabbed the stick and threw it in reverse, released the air brakes with a big whoosh, slammed on the accelerator, and we spun gravel out of the parking lot.

"Hey! Stop, you clowns!" Jean came hurtling back down the steps. "Or I'll tear your faces off!" But we didn't stop. Not at all. We tore down the street, heading for Eastlake and back to the Dirt Club, going about sixty in a thirty mph zone. The bus went a lot faster than Veronica could. Howie was in doggie heaven. He stuck his head out the window and barked and drooled at all the cars going the other way.

We headed south on Eastlake and were about as far as the Lakeview Boulevard off-ramp, when the siren started up behind us. Ziggy went running to the back of the bus.

"It's those chick cops, man! Step on the gas!"

Horns began honking behind us.

"Oh, my God—it's Thompson! And Marjorie Mamet, and Jean, the sado/maso/psycho-killer bus driver! They're all after us!"

I put the pedal to the metal, as the truck drivers say, and we screamed down the next six blocks to the light at Denny, ran the light, took the corner on one-and-a-half wheels, hurtled down the alley, and came to a screeching halt outside the loading dock of the erstwhile Dirt Club. The squad car siren wailed bansheelike close behind. I flipped open the bus door.

"Let's go, Zig! Once we get inside, we can lose ourselves in the crowd. They'll never find us in there!"

"Yeah—except when we go onstage to perform," Zig countered.

We ran through the alley entrance into the club, Howie close on our heels.

It was deafening inside. And dark. And very, very crowded. They were on a break between bands and were playing something really loud by Harm's Donkeys.

"Let's hustle," I hollered to Ziggy. "We've gotta find the others. I think we have to go on in about five minutes!"

Suddenly, there was a commotion at the front door, rising above all the other commotion. I looked through the crowd and the smoke and the darkness to see a large clump of people pushing past the bouncer at the front door—Mr. Thompson, Marjorie Mamet, Jean the bus driver, and Officers Ratched and Waters. Their eyes scanned the crowd.

"We're busted!" Ziggy hollered. "Big time!"

Just then, with a crackle and a hiss, we heard Lewd's voice come over the microphone: "Are right, you guys! That was Harm's Donkeys' new EP, 'What Girl?' Awesome and I don't mean maybe! The next band on the lineup was supposed to be DogBreath, but two of their members can't be found anywhere. So we'll skip down the list to the next group on the contest lineup—the odds-on favorite to win tonight—the Angry Housewives! So let's hear it for the Housewives!"

"Wait a minute! Wait a minute! Stop! We're here! We're here!" cried Ziggy. He started pushing through the dense crowd toward the backstage. I shoved along behind him, and so did Howie. Somewhere in this crowd were a couple of cops, two bureauocratnik teachers, and a sado/maso/psycho-killer forty-five-year-old bus driver, searching for us. It lent a sense of urgency to our movements.

We broke through to the backstage area and found the tiny dressing cubicle next to the women's bathroom. Weasel ghosted over, staring balefully over our heads.

"Where have you guys been! You are so on the sugar beet list!" Or words to that effect.

Todi and Flipper stood there, glaring at us as usual. Phoebe stood off to one side behind them, staring off into space.

"Man, I'm—I'm gonna have to talk fast," Weasel continued, "but I think I can get Fingers to reschedule you guys after this Housewives thing. You guys, you guys, you don't wanna blow this. It's money, man—it's the big time!"

Ziggy pushed his way forward. "Oh, man, I know, it's a drag—I had to go and get my lucky dress, and there was a lot of sort of legal hassles—"

Lewd's voice came over the house speaker system: "Come on, can we go, the Angry Housewives?"

"Hi, Tim, honey," said my mom. I looked and there was my mom, all dressed up, holding her guitar, with a lost look on her face. Standing next to her were Jetta and Mrs. Lewis, looking like something had died.

"Mom, they're calling you guys. Get up there on stage. Let's not have two failures in the family."

"We can't go on," said my mom. "Wendy's not here. We can't find her anywhere."

"Let's face the facts, Bev," said Mrs. Lewis. "She flaked out on us *again*. She's always had a fear of success. Oh, well, I guess it takes a crisis to figure out who your friends are. Let's go home, ladies."

"You're right," said my mom. She pulled off her blond wig and threw it on the floor. "And I said I was going to lighten up. What a joke."

"I don't want to go!" protested Jetta. "I want to sing! I like this band! In fact, I *love* this band! I don't want to go back to my old life!"

I became aware of a growing rumble from the crowd out front. Lewd Fingers came bursting offstage, his eyes wild.

"What the hell is the holdup back here? That crowd is going insane. Are you guys going on, or what? Carol?"

"We're not going on, Lewd. Sorry. Get real, Jetta. It's not happening. There's no Wendy. There's no band."

"Oh, yes, there is," I said. "Gimme your drumsticks, Ziggy." I snatched the drumsticks out of his hip pocket and headed for the women's bathroom. There were four girls inside, including, of course, Suzie Blethins and her dear ex-best friend, Karen Olson.

"Tim! What are you guys doing in the girls' bathroom? Get out of here!"

Ziggy came lurching in after me. "What are you doing with my sticks, dude?" he demanded.

"I'm drumming for the Housewives. Give me your dress."

"What??"

"I said, give me your dress. I need it. They've been all

over the media as an all-chick band—it's part of their gimmick. I need to look like a chick!"

"No! You can't have my dress. This is my lucky dress. And—wait—if you go on with the Housewives, you can't go on with DogBreath!"

"Why not?" I said.

"Because you'd be competing against yourself, nor-Brain. Conflict of interestissimo."

"We'll take it a step at a time," I said. "Now give me that dress!" I snatched at the garment in dispute. Ziggy yanked it away. I socked him in the nose, and he crumpled to the ground, moaning. Suzie screamed. I grabbed the dress, shucked off my clothes, and slipped it on. "Sorry, Ziggy my pal. Zip me," I growled at Suzie.

"I can't believe it. They're fighting over a dress," drawled Karen Olson, looking in the mirror and fixing her lipstick.

"Shut up, sheep dog head," I snarled. "And give me your damn lipstick!" I snatched a tube of Scarlet Pimpernel out of her hand and slathered it on my manly lips. Somebody else had left a bottle of liquid eyeliner on the shelf by the mirror. I slopped some around my eyes. Huh, I thought to myself. Interesting look. Kinda hostile. I headed back outside. Ziggy crawled to his feet and stumbled along behind me.

The Housewives stood there in a forlorn group, Still Life with Lewd.

"Tim, you look so pretty," said my mom.

"Let's go, ladies," I said.

"Go where?" asked Jetta.

"Onstage. They're calling for the Angry Housewives."

Lewd looked at me like a lizard, blinking his seemingly lidless eyes.

"Nice gesture, kid. But I can't let you play in two bands. You'd be competing against yourself. No can do."

"I don't care," I said. "Forget DogBreath. It's history anyway. I'm going on with the Housewives. There's no rule that says you have to be a girl to be in the band."

"You can't do this to us, Timmer!" pleaded Zig. "You *are* DogBreath. You don't play, we don't win!"

"There's too much pressure to change things in the group. I liked it the way it was. I'm not interested anymore."

My mother looked at me, very focused, very intense. "This is a big chance for you, honey. I guess I never really believed it, but you have a chance to take your music and make something happen for yourself and your friends. I don't want you to do something you'll regret later."

Jetta and Mrs. Lewis stared at me.

"Yeah, for Dog's sake, Threll, what the hell, you're throwing us over for a chick band?" said Flipper.

"Sorry, you guys. You wanted out anyway."

"Well, somebody do something!" hollered Lewd. "I've got a hostile crowd out there. They're gonna start throwing stuff pretty soon if we don't get a band up on that stage!"

I leaned down and picked up my mom's blond wig and pulled it on. Suddenly a familiar voice cried, "There's one of them now! And the dog!"

Mr. Thompson and Officers Waters and Ratched came running around the back of the stage. They looked right past me, never recognized me at all. Ziggy took one look and fled around into the crowd. The police and the counselor gave chase.

Suddenly two other very tall women pushed their way through the crowd. They both carried drumsticks. The brunette was dressed for success in a pinstripe dress suit. The blonde had on something Hawaiian.

Lewd looked at them. "Who are you guys?"

"I'm going on for Wendy," said the blonde.

"*I'm* going on for Wendy," said the brunette, shoving the blonde away and heading for the stage.

"I don't know who you guys are," I said, "but *I'm* going on for Wendy, and that's the way it is!"

"Tim?" said the brunette in a deep voice.

"That's Tim?" said the blonde. "Somehow I pictured him as a guy."

"Get outta my way," I said. "I gotta go on."

"I'm going on," said the brunette. "I'm Wendy's boy-friend, Wally!"

"Well, I'm Jetta Prince's husband, Larry, and she's the lead singer, so *I'm* going on!" said the blonde, taking a swing at the brunette. The brunette ducked. Just at that moment, Jean, the bus driver, came running by, and Larry Prince's fist connected with Jean's jaw. Jean went down like a sack of instant potatoes.

"Ow!" said Larry, shaking his fist. "Ow!"

"Larry?" said Jetta. "Larry? Honey, you bought a dress and everything? I thought you hated this band!"

"I did, I do. But you're more important to me than my feelings or my job. Do you really like this outfit? Dolce and Gabbana. Mother got it half price in Lord & Taylor's basement."

"Oh, Larry, I love you," said Jetta.

"You guys, I'm here, I'm sorry, I'm sorry!"

Our heads spun around. There was Wendy, in costume and out of breath.

"Wendy!" shrieked the Housewives in unison.

"I'm sorry. I flaked out on you guys. Am I too late? Can I still be in the band?"

"Yes!" they chorused.

"Thank God!" said Lewd. He went running out on stage and grabbed the mike.

"And here they are at last, the group you've been waiting for—the Angry Housewives!"

My mom took a last look at me before she went onstage. "Tim, honey?"

"Yeah?"

"I love you. This was a really nice gesture—offering to play for us. Thank you."

"I love you, too, Mom. You're awesome. Give 'em hell."

My mom and her three friends ran onstage, and the crowd went wild.

A half hour later, after the commotion had died down, there was only one band left on the lineup. DogBreath. I didn't even care anymore. The evening belonged, once again, to the Angry Housewives. I was nobody. Todi and

Flipper had long since stomped out. Ziggy was nowhere to be seen—for all I knew, Officers Ratched and Waters had taken him to jail for vandalism, and they'd probably be back for me as an accessory or aiding and abetting or something like that. I didn't even care about that. I'd washed my face and put back on my own black clothing.

Still, when I heard Lewd's voice over the microphone, saying, "And now, for the last band of the evening, I give you DogBreath!" a chill ran up my spine. Except, except, of course, there was no DogBreath. I sat slumped backstage. There were a few moments of silence. Then, over the PA system, I heard the familiar strumming of an acoustic guitar. I jumped up and peered out through the backstage curtains. Phoebe stood alone onstage in a single spotlight. She stood at the front microphone, strumming the intro to "Boys Don't Care." She looked so lonely and forlorn. She sang, in her weird breathy little voice:

> "Girls don't care about your hair
> 'Bout what you wear, about your car
> Girls just care 'bout who you are
> Inside."

Someone had left a Gibson electric leaning against the bank of amplifiers onstage. I walked on and plugged it into the amp. I stood back in the shadows and began to play along.

Phoebe glanced back at me, and kept going. I stepped in closer to a microphone that had been set up for a backup vocalist.

Suddenly, a drum fill snapped my attention. I looked over to the drum kit upstage. There was Ziggy, looking kind of even more roughed up than usual, even with his lucky dress on. He gave me a pleading look, I nodded, and he started leaning into the rhythm section.

Phoebe went on. I started singing backup with her.

"Girls just want to take you higher
Than the moon above you
Boys just want to break your heart
They don't want to love you"

I, lost in the song, suddenly pulled up short when a blistering guitar solo that wasn't me, split the air. There on the stage, standing in the middle, lost in the ozone, playing like some maniac Buddhist angel, was Doctor Killboy Powerhead. His fingers practically had flames shooting out of them. The crowd, which had been trancing out, suddenly went in-totally-freaking-sane. Then he nodded to me. Ziggy started crashing into a manic drum cross-hand riff, Phoebe wailed to her music goddesses. I ran over next to Doctor Powerhead, and we did power guitar metal duet #67—the Heart Chakra Conflagration Face-Off. If I die tomorrow, I'll die happy. It was my peak experience.

Out there in the crowd, I saw familiar faces—my mother and her friends, surrounded by many new friends. Jean, the bus driver, conscious once more. Officers Waters and Ratched. Mr. Thompson and Mr. Fredericks. Suzie Blethins, and her ex-ex-friend Karen. They were all smiling.

When the song was finished, the crowd at the Dirt Club was silent for a full minute before they erupted into a huge, pandemonium lovefest aimed right at Phoebe.

My personal heart was also experiencing a majorly unexpected love fest, also aimed right at Pheebs. I crossed the stage. Phoebe stood alone in the spotlight, holding on to her guitar, stunned by the power of what was happening to her, the audience response. I felt all these warm feelings in my heart for Phoebe. I wanted to take her in my arms, kiss her, hold her, hold her, hold her, hold her, hold her to my throbbing, overwhelmed self.

There are times, they say, when time stands still. This was one of those times. I crossed the stage, slowly, like in a dream, or a TV football instant replay, the roaring of the crowd like the roar of far-off ocean surf in my lovestruck ears. I heard myself saying out loud, "I love you, Phoebe! I love you!"

Right before I got to her, Jason Haley came slithering onstage, went up to Phoebe, took her by the arm, and steered her offstage.

And that is how DogBreath won the second contest.

Chapter Twenty-three

So DogBreath won the contest. Only it wasn't starring me, the way the plan was supposed to go. It was starring Phoebe and Doctor Powerhead. I believe that's what Mrs. Cederberg, my English Lit teacher, would call irony.* Because not only has my band been taken over by Other People, one of the people who took it over is this girl who goes off with a sophisticated and slimy record producer the minute I discover I'm in love with her myself.

To ease the pain, I tried to write a song about Phoebe, except there isn't much that rhymes with "Phoebe" except totally stupid stuff like "heebie jeebies" and "jujubes" and "seabees" and "peevees."

She's been leaving me phone messages at my mom's house. But I don't want her pity. Winners can't understand the pain of losers. They may think they can, but they can't.

*See Chapter One.

* * *

I and Ziggy only had to stay in jail for about a day and half, on a variety of specious charges ranging from breaking and entering to unlawfully driving a school bus. We have been ordered to perform community service—play every Wednesday for six months at the Seattle Center Senior Citizen's Dance. Merengue. Cha-cha-cha.

Ziggy doesn't care—he's just totally thrilled that Dog-Breath won the contest. He'd probably play drums for Up With People if he thought it would make him famous. I just haven't told him yet that we're probably not in the band anymore. He's my best friend kind of. I don't want to hurt him.

Mom's house is total chaos, what with the media, and record executives, and photographers, and the phone ringing off the hook. Looks like Angry Housewives is going to be monster. I got mobbed my first day back in school. And of course Suzie's trying to be nice to me since I was on TV. I'm so over her. I made barfing motions toward her last time she tried to talk to me.

Where I will go from here, I don't know. I'm feeling totally lost. So I write an extremely emotional twelve-page letter to the Universe—I express all of my anger and angst and resentment and regret and emptiness and outrage and loss to the lady in the fur bikini. I decide to take my letter down to the Raquel Welch Memorial Bridge Mailbox, burn it, and scatter the ashes on the lake below, releasing my anguish to the silent waters in their slow, unending voyage to the eternal Sea.

I walk down the hill to the bridge. It's a late winter day, blowy, gray, birds tumbling through the sky, paper skittering down the sidewalk, the violins of sadness playing in my heart.

My coat collar's turned up, my hands in my pocket, wind in my face. An orange cat follows me for half a block then disappears into the blackberry bushes. The wet, weedy smell of the lake comes curling through the wind. I look out across Lake Union. People flying kites over in Gasworks Park. Sailboats and barges plowing majestically through the cut under the bridge. Life Going On. Violins of sadness.

As I near the mailbox, I sense my life coming to the River of No Return. From this day on, nothing will ever be the same, and I will be merely a sadly comic footnote in a mirror tragedy of this artistically boozhy age. I heave a sigh and open the mailbox door.

There's an envelope inside. A letter to the bridge, probably. I pull it out. It smells of roses. It's addressed to "Tim." That must be me. I've mailed so many letters to the Universe at this mailbox, and the Universe is finally getting around to answering me? I open it, mystified.

A greeting card inside. I read the following:

Dear Tim:
Thank you for letting me be in your band. It has been fun and educational, but I think it has not been very much fun for you. Ziggy was the

one who made me be in the band and the other members and you didn't like me very much and it is my fault that your original band broke up.

Jason Haley from Chainsaw Records wanted me to quit DogBreath and go with him to make a new band called DogBreath with just me and Doctor Powerhead and some different new people, but I told him it wasn't fair because you and Ziggy started DogBreath and besides you wrote most of the songs and are the actual lead singer and it was only because of you that I started to sing or write any songs.

So they are going to give you a recording contract but I will not be in the album because I do not think it is fair to you. Even though they want to record "Boy's Don't Care" which you helped me write as well as your songs such as "Hell School" and "Better and Better. "

I'm going to try to go away from your life now for both our sakes, but I didn't want to go without saying it to you first so you would know...which otherwise it wouldn't be fair.

Sincerely yours, your friend
Phoebe Fortiere

At that moment I had a very important realization about myself. Which was: I am a complete and total jerk and should be killed.

I saw a figure coming slowly toward me from the end

of the bridge. A small blond person in a long blue coat that flapped in the breeze. Carrying a guitar case. Phoebe. I looked down, not trusting myself. She stopped a few yards away from me.

"Hi, Tib."

I didn't say anything.

"Um, I just wondered if you would maybe listen to this one song I'm trying to write," she whispered. "Before I go out of your life."

I accidentally looked into Phoebe's eyes. They were so blue. They were dark deep blue oceans. The lake breeze blew her baby duck feathers hair across her face. In a little rush, the song I'd been trying to write fell into place.

"Oh, Phoebe, Phoebe," I recited,
"Springtime without you would tot-
al agony be."

There was a long silence. A deep, long blast from a far-off tug boat reverberated through the bright air.

"That was a haiku," she said.

"Seventeen syllables," I said. "Five, seven, five, right?"

"You wrote me a haiku."

"Yeah. I did."

"Thank you, Tibby." She looked out over the lake.

I waited a few moments. I couldn't tell what she was thinking. "So what's the name of your song, Pheeb?" I asked.

"Evil Spirits and Their Secretaries."

I looked at her, so kind of vulnerable and serious and clueless. "Well, come on, then. Let's go over to Ziggy's place and you can play it for me."

"Okay," she said.

"Because if we're going to record an album we're going to need a bunch more songs. We better get started, huh?"

Phoebe looked at me carefully through her blue plastic glasses.

"I guess we better."

"I just have to stop on the way over to Zig's and pick up some Tang and peanut butter. He's all out."

"Okay," she said.

A flock of sparrows suddenly exploded out of a bare maple tree on the lake shore and flew north, trilling madly, on the spring wind. I closed the door on the Raquel Welch Memorial Bridge Mailbox. I held out my hand, Phoebe took it, and we started up the hill beneath the racing April clouds.

My life is getting better and better.